Stolen Heart

Ivy Marie

Ivy Marie Publishing

STOLEN HEART

Contents

Prologue

Noah

"Aiden." I entered my friend's apartment. "I brought you something to eat."

Aiden didn't say anything. Setting the Chinese on the kitchen's breakfast bar, I scanned the space. Aiden stood by the large window in his living room. Concerned, I moved closer.

"Aiden? You should eat."

"I'm not hungry." Aiden said without turning from the window.

"When was the last time you ate?" I prodded.

"I'm not hungry." He repeated — the words hollow sounding.

"You're looking pretty thin, my friend."

"You are not my friend." Aiden's voice hardened. "A friend wouldn't keep me from my love."

I scowled at him through the reflection of the glass. "She's not your love."

My friend turned a glare on me. There was something in his gaze, an unnatural glimmer that had nothing to do with him being a warlock. My gut tightened. That look unnerved me.

Taking hold of Aiden's arm, I tugged him toward the kitchen. Stubbornly he planted his feet. I stumbled forward at the sudden stop.

1

Aiden simultaneously yanked his arm from my grip and shot me with a spell just as I was turning to face him. I flew back into the corner of the breakfast bar. I wasn't sure what hurt more — the corner to my back or the spell to my front. It didn't matter. Pain radiated throughout my body, and my friend was trying to make a break for it.

"I don't think so." I growled through the pain.

Pushing myself away from the bar, I wrapped my arms around Aiden as he reached for the door handle. Wolf beats warlock anytime in physical strength. This is the first time I've ever had to use any force since he's started acting oddly. I hauled him back into the apartment.

"Let me go, beast!" Aiden kicked and squirmed, trying to get out of my grip.

I ignored the insult, knowing he was not in his right mind. It was a struggle — mostly on his part — but I returned to the living room. With my belt, I tied him to the coffee table. A temporary fix, it won't hold him for long. I went in search of something better. I shifted through boxes in a storage room, finding bungee cords, extension cords, and Christmas lights.

"This should work."

Returning to the living room, I undid the ties, moving Aiden from the floor to a chair. Using the lights, I tied him to it. I raised the footrest, used extension cords to tie his legs down, and then closed the footrest.

"You need help." I told him.

"I need my love."

"I'll find you some help."

"All I need is Rosetta."

I let out a low growl. "I'll be back soon."

"You can't understand my heartbreak." Aiden laughed darkly. "But you will."

Those ominous words sent a chill down my spine. It didn't sound like my friend at all. Whatever was happening to him was getting worse. Taking a towel from the kitchen, I gagged him. I felt terrible for leaving him this way, but I'll feel worse if something happens to him while in this condition.

Chapter One

Noah

S tepping out of the car, I double-checked the address on my phone. A four-storey brick apartment building stood before me. Nothing about the building gave me confidence that I'd found someone to help.

Seeing my distress after returning home from Aiden's last night, fellow pack member Julianne suggested I come here. She told me that a very skilled tracker lives in this apartment building. I am skeptical that I need a tracker. Maybe, all I need is a healer. But Julianne insisted I tell my problem to this tracker. So here I am, outside the tracker's apartment, wondering if this is the right choice. Aiden is the only healer that I know. Maybe this tracker knows another healer that can help me.

'And in other news.'

I could hear the news anchor through the paper-thin walls of the apartments I passed.

'Police are still looking for the men in connection to the murders that occurred at the recent rave. They ask the public to keep their eyes open for the suspects and to call the police with any information.'

The noise muted itself when I stepped into the elevator. The rickety box opened on the fourth floor. I stepped out, sniffing the air. Julianne warned me that this tracker is a former pack member and may hesitate to help. I followed the scent of a wolf to the end of the hall. I paused at the door, not knowing who I was about to face. The image of Aiden floated in my mind reminding me why I was here. Raising a hand, I knocked on the flimsy wooden door and waited.

"Yes?"

The door opened a crack, stopped only by a security chain. A partial face of a woman in sunglasses peered out at me. I thought Julianne had tricked me, and then I considered this woman could be the tracker's girlfriend.

"I'm looking for the tracker." I told her.

"What do you want?"

"It's a matter I'd rather discuss with the tracker."

She frowned. The door closed, and I heard the chain slide away before the door opened wider. I stared down at the petite brunette with red undertones. She was a good head shorter than me, curvy, and breathtaking. My body — and wolf — reacted immediately. The simple jeans and t-shirt accentuated every curve, curves my hands itched to roam over her body. I also wanted to reach out and remove those sunglasses so I could see what colour her eyes were.

"Are you coming in?"

"Yes." I shook my head to clear it of lusty thoughts of this woman and stepped into the tiny entry space. "My name is Noah."

"Eve."

I have never reacted this way to a woman before. She closed the door behind me, putting locks back in place, then led me down the short entry hall to the open-concept apartment. Directly in front of me was the kitchen, and to the right, a single couch and chair angled toward an old TV. The apartment is dark, blinds cover the windows, and the light fixtures cast a dim yellow glow on the rest of the apartment. She gestured for me to take a seat.

I sat on the couch anxiously. This tiny woman made me anxious. I'm the Alpha, I shouldn't be nervous around anyone, yet this woman made me feel... unworthy.

And those sunglasses. Those sunglasses of hers were unnerving. I can smell she's a wolf, so she must know I'm one too. I wondered if she wore those sunglasses to hide the unnatural glow from being a wolf. Some wolves sit so close to the surface that it shows in the eyes. If that's true, she should be in the pack.

Eve stopped at the kitchen briefly to fill two glasses of water. Coming over, she handed one to me before settling in the chair.

"Thank you." I took the glass and placed it on the coffee table.

"What does a wolf want with me?" She asked coolly. "Did the Alpha send you?"

I remembered what Julianne told me to say. "A friend suggested you may be able to help me."

"What friend?"

"Julianne."

Eve stiffened but nodded. "What do you need me to track?"

"I'm not sure." I admitted.

The slightest show of irritation crossed her features. "How can you not be sure?"

"Let me explain. A couple of months ago, my best friend started seeing someone. It was casual and simple — coffee dates, easy dinners, that kind of thing." I paused with a nonchalant wave of my hand. "Roughly two weeks ago, he told me he broke it off because she was becoming too clingy. Then suddenly, while we were having lunch, he changed."

"Changed how?" She questioned cautiously.

"He started pinning for his ex. Saying things like she has his heart and he needs her to survive."

Eve stared at me for a full minute before speaking. "Is your friend a wolf like you?"

"Aiden? No, he's a warlock."

"And this woman, the ex, do you know her name?"

"He called her Rosetta."

Her jaw tightened. "Did you let him go to her?"

"No." I shook my head. "I noticed a strange glow in his eyes last night that concerned me. That's why I'm here. Other wise I've been keeping him in his apartment."

"Let me see him."

I blinked at her. "Excuse me?"

"Your warlock friend may be in more danger than you know. I need to see him."

I didn't argue. My gut tightened with dread, fearing she may be right. With a curt nod, I stood. Eve followed me out, locking her apartment behind us. Taking the stairs, I hurried down them, anxious to return to Aiden's side. At the bottom, I turned, realizing Eve wasn't directly behind me. With a hand on the railing and her head angled downward, she took the steps one at a time.

She insisted on seeing Aiden, yet she took her sweet time descending those stairs. It took all my willpower not to be tapping my foot impatiently. Aiden needs me. When she finally hit the bottom, I opened the door to the building. She moved faster out the door than she did going down those stairs.

I opened the passenger door helping Eve inside, before rushing to the driver's side. I glanced at her from the corner of my eye. Eve's leg bounced, and she nibbled on her thumbnail. The nervous gesture made me curious, but it wasn't my place to ask. I'm a client. I think. She hasn't officially accepted my request, and we haven't discussed any payment terms unless she will help me because I'm pack.

I parked at Aiden's building. The difference between Eve's brick building and Aiden's glass high rise is glaring. Helping Eve out of the car, I vaguely wondered what she thought when those who appeared better off than her asked for help. Again, it's not my place.

Eve gripped the handrail in the elevator as we rode up to the twenty-third floor. I raised a brow at her, but she didn't notice. Or maybe she was ignoring me. She is not obligated to answer any of the personal questions I'm dying to ask.

"I tied Aiden to a chair." I explained, using my spare key to enter the apartment. "He was getting more desperate to leave. Even hit me with a spell."

I opened the door, gesturing for Eve to enter. She walked ahead of me. My eyes drifted to her swaying hips and shapely ass. I held in a groan. This woman, without any effort, is testing my control. My wolf was whining at me for not making a move on her. He wanted me to kiss her, strip her of her clothes, and get her into bed. I want the same thing, but now is not the time to act on primal desires.

A strangled sound drew me from my lusty thoughts of Eve. Closing the door, I rushed to Aiden's side. He was foaming around the gag.

I pulled it out so he could breathe better. Eve stared down at him emotionless.

"What's happening?"

"I don't know." I admitted, panicked.

"What's wrong?"

"Are you blind?" I snapped, glaring at Eve. "Aiden is foaming at the mouth."

Her lips pulled into a tight smile. Reaching up, she lowered her sunglasses to the bridge of her nose. I stared dumbfounded. Stormy grey eyes stared back at me. Various shades of grey swirled over a cloudy surface. It wasn't just her pupils but the whole eyes. It was mesmerizing and beautiful.

"I've been blind for five years."

She replaced her sunglasses, and I shook myself out of a trance. I regretted snapping at her. My wolf paced in my head. I could feel his need to go after the person who blinded her.

"I'm sorry." I whispered, not sure what to say.

"It's not your fault." She shrugged nonchalantly. "You said he's foaming at the mouth?"

"Yes."

"Grab your friend. There's a doctor I know who may be able to help."

The neighbourhood Eve had me drive to is run down. I found it hard to believe a doctor would work in this area. The street lamps that did work flickered in an attempt to stay lit, garbage bags overflowed from dumpsters, and many buildings looked like they should be condemned. Homeless slept in doorways, women of the night walking down the street looked sickly, and I think I might have driven past a drug deal.

"Are you sure this doctor can help?" I questioned, wanting to get out of this neighbourhood as quicky as possible.

"Maybe." Eve shrugged. "He'll need to examine your friend to be sure."

Reluctantly I parked beside the building that this doctor worked out off. I almost threw up at the putrid scent of piss and unwashed bodies when I opened my car door. Eve was already out of the car and took the three steps from the sidewalk to the front door. I rushed to collect Aiden and followed her. Eve knocked on the solid-looking door of the building, and a small window slid open to reveal beady eyes.

"The blind can see." Eve stated cryptically.

The window closed. I could hear the sound of locks clicking before the door swung open. A large, heavy-set man with cropped black hair ushered us inside.

He smiled widely at Eve. "You're a sight to behold."

"Love to catch up." She reached up, patting his chest. "But this is an emergency."

The man's smile vanished. "What's wrong?"

"Heartless."

A sense of urgency filled the air. "Room three. I'll get the doctor."

"Thanks, Will."

10

Locks were put back in place before the man — Will — rushed off. Eve took me upstairs. At the top, she stepped aside, reminding me what room Will told us to go to. Taking the lead, I opened the second door on the left. The room reminded me of a dentist's rather than a doctor's office.

"Put Aiden in the chair and restrain him."

I followed Eve's instructions. A leather band buckled around his chest and legs, and individual ones bound his wrists to the chair arms. Aiden had stopped moving at some point during the drive. I pressed my fingers to his neck, relieved to find a pulse.

Eve took a seat near the door. Her leg bounced, and she nibbled on her thumbnail again. Again I wondered what made her so nervous. Despite the current situation, looking at her put me and my wolf at ease.

Hurried footsteps could be heard from down the hall. The door flung open, drawing the attention of Eve and myself. A man with blond hair, glasses, a pink shirt, a white lab coat, jeans and flip-flops surveyed the room. His eyes are what caught my attention. Like Aiden, the green flecks within the blue of his iris sparked with magic.

He saw me, saw Aiden, but focused on Eve. Kneeling, he took her face in his hands. "Darling, tell me you're all right."

Chapter Two

Eve

I sat anxiously in the room with Noah and Aiden, waiting for Dr. Twin. Five years. I never imagined Rosetta would return. This time the Heartless witch targeted a warlock. As horrible as it is that Aiden is Rosetta's newest victim, I can't help but be grateful for this opportunity. This is my chance to redeem myself.

Rosetta isn't my only issue. I've had to adapt to a suddenly grey world for five years. My sense of smell and hearing heightened with the lack of vision. Then Noah knocked on my door, bringing the scent of pine needles and sunshine. I could see Noah far more clearly than anything else. He's still grey but a lighter grey. I can see the individual fingers on his hands.

I could feel my skin prickle with awareness whenever Noah looked at me. Even my wolf took notice. She's been dormant for so long. It's an odd feeling having her consciousness merge with mine again. Noah did this to me. If not for the opportunity to track down Rosetta, I would have kicked him out of my apartment, scared of what he stirs inside me.

Hurried footsteps could be heard from the hall. The door flinging open startled me. My first instinct was fear, fear that Rosetta found

Aiden, but then the scent of rosemary hit me. I relaxed, knowing the figure in the door was Dr. Twin. He knelt and cupped my face.

"Darling, tell me you're all right."

"I'm fine."

Oddly I sensed Noah's annoyance at the doctor when he cupped my face. Or maybe it was something else. It felt primal. I removed Dr. Twin's hands. Jerking my chin toward Noah, I introduced the two men. Dr. Twin sucked in a sharp breath of air. I heard the whistled hiss as it passed through his teeth.

"My, my, what a specimen."

I bit the inside of my cheek to keep from smiling. "Noah is my client."

"You're no fun."

"Eve said you may be able to help." Noah stated, doubt lacing his tone.

"And that voice." Dr. Twin sighed heavily. "Darling, you've outdone yourself."

I also like the low timber of Noah's voice. "Aiden is your patient."

"Let me see what we have."

Dr. Twin moved away from me. I heard the snapping of latex gloves and knew he was examining Aiden. I kept my eyes on Noah. His anxiety over his friend seeped into me. I know there's no saving Aiden unless we give him to Rosetta, or I can find the Heartless Witch before it's too late.

"What's the timeline?" Dr. Twin demanded.

"Timeline?" Noah repeated.

"Foaming started today." I answered. "Roughly two weeks ago, he started acting oddly."

"That's right." Noah added. "He was seeing someone for two months before that."

"Hmm." Dr. Twin mused.

"Hmm?" Noah questioned, repeating the sound. "What does that mean?"

"I'm afraid there's not much I can do."

With that solemn statement, the room went quiet. I heard the distinct sound of Dr. Twin removing the latex gloves and could feel Noah's anger rising. If Dr. Twin can't do much, my timeline to find the Heartless Witch is short. Too short. Fear twisted my stomach. I don't want to lose another person to that witch.

"What can you do?" I asked, hopeful for anything.

"The best I can do is put him in a magically induced coma state." Dr. Twin stated. "It'll only be a temporary stop, not a permanent fix."

"For how long?"

Dr. Twin didn't answer. I raised my voice, asking the question again, needing an answer.

"For how long?"

"A week. But, Darling, I don't want you going after this witch."

"I have to." I stated softly.

"What witch?" Noah demanded. "Is Aiden going to die? What are you two not telling me?"

I stared at Noah's pale grey form, forgetting he was in the room momentarily. "Dr. Twin, can you give Noah a check-up?"

"Check-up? What for?"

"Make sure she didn't get to him too."

"My pleasure." Dr. Twin answered gleefully.

I stood and left the room. The sound reduction magic cast on the room didn't reduce the sounds of items crashing against the door. I smiled faintly. It reminded me of my first check-up with the doctor. Adam brought me long after Alpha Jack had rescued me from an abusive Alpha. I was more comfortable with others by this point, but Dr. Twin's flamboyant nature scared me. I threw everything within reach at him to keep him at bay. The doctor had convinced me that he could complete the check-up with me in wolf form, I accepted those terms because I didn't feel as vulnerable as a wolf, and he talked through every step of the check-up.

I slid to the floor next to the door, lost in memories of the past. Something touched my knee, jolting me out of the past and into the present. My heart pounded as I pressed myself against the wall, away from the sizeable grey form in front of me.

"Eve, it's me." The voice soothed.

As my senses returned to the present, my mind recognized that voice. The warm nutmeg scent confirmed the identity.

"Will."

"Are you okay?" He asked, concern in his tone.

"I'm fine. I was reminiscing about my first check-up with the doctor."

Will went silent for a moment. "Is Dr. Twin giving that man you came with a check-up?"

"Yep. I wanted to make sure Heartless didn't do anything to Noah."

"Wise decision."

Using the wall at my back, I stood. "Can never be too careful."

"So." Will elongated the vowel. "Is this Noah person your new boyfriend?"

"Client." I answered quickly.

"You're going to let your beauty go to waste."

"Beauty is only skin deep."

"Inside and out, Eve."

Will has a unique ability to see inside people's souls. He's claimed, since day one, that mine is beautiful. We've done this banter before. This is the first time he's questioned me about a boyfriend since I lost Adam. It made me curious.

"What do you see in Noah?"

"Curious, are we?"

Before I could answer, the door slammed open. Noah's pine scent assaulted my nose. Irritation washed off him in waves. Dr. Twin's check-up diagnosis couldn't have been that bad.

"Let's go." Noah growled.

"Don't be a stranger." Dr. Twin cooed. "Darling, he's quite the specimen."

"You can trust him." Will stated.

I pushed off the wall to follow Noah. He didn't wait for me. He was already outside by the time I made it down the stairs. Opening the door, I scowled at the night sky. Since losing my sight, nighttime has become my enemy. Everything in my gray vision darkens, so I can barely see the shapes around me.

Dr. Twin has three steps from the door to the sidewalk. Putting my hands out, I searched for the handrail I knew was there. Somewhere. Gripping it tightly, I carefully slid one foot until it caught the edge and stepped down.

"Here."

Noah's large hands gripped my waist. He lifted me and placed me safely on the sidewalk. I sucked in a breath when he touched me. His touch warmed my skin through my clothes. Noah didn't let me go immediately after placing me on the sidewalk. Instead, I felt his hands tighten on my waist.

"Thanks." I mumbled.

"I'll take you home." Noah said, his voice sounding strained.

He slid his hand to my back and ushered me away from Dr. Twin's building. His hand tightened in my shirt, stopping me abruptly. I heard the car door open, and he helped me inside before closing the door. I felt cold with the loss of Noah's touch. I shifted in my seat, uncomfortable with the odd feeling.

"Your doctor friend is... interesting." Noah stated after entering the car himself.

"He's a lot to take in on the first visit." My lips quirked upward. "But he's good at what he does."

"Which is what exactly?"

I shrugged. "He's a doctor. He helps those who can't go to a hospital."

"You don't know the details do you?" He sounded amused.

Bristling, I crossed my arms. "How did the check-up go?"

Noah growled. "Aiden hit me with a spell that affects my heart. It could slow down dangerously if I don't keep it stimulated."

"Stimulated? So, with exercise?"

"Yeah." He drew out the word. "With exercise."

"That shouldn't be too hard for you. If I recall, all male wolves love to exercise."

Noah snorted. "Not all males."

I didn't think much of his reaction and continued speaking as if he didn't interrupt me. "Is Dr. Twin able to reverse the spell?"

"He'll look into it."

Noah then fell silent. We stayed silent for a while. I feel comfortable with Noah. It's an odd feeling. Adam was the last person who made me this comfortable. My wolf whined, urging me to get closer to him. I wrapped my arms around myself, resisting her nudging in my mind. I need to keep things professional with Noah. Once I deal with Rosetta, he'll be on his way.

"What's the next step?" Noah questioned.

I jumped, startled to hear his voice. "I'm going to track down the woman."

"Rosetta."

I nodded.

"How are you going to track her?"

"I'll sleep on it."

"How can I help?"

"There's nothing you can do right now."

The car came to a complete stop, and the engine shut off. I assumed we were parked in front of my apartment building.

"Will you tell me when you need help?" Noah asked.

Will I? I'm not sure. Clients should stay out of my way. They don't typically provide much aid. Noah, as a wolf, could. Except his scent will be a distraction. So, I probably won't tell him if I need help. I got out of the car without answering him. There's nothing to say.

My apartment building is well-lit, the outside lights illuminating my path to the front door. I didn't need Noah to follow me, but he did — with a hand on my back, opening doors, and helping me up the stairs.

"This was unnecessary." I told him.

"What was unnecessary?"

"Guiding me to my apartment."

"I wanted to."

My heart jumped at that statement. It shouldn't have. I need distance. Unlocking the door, I slipped inside. Noah's hand slammed against the door when I tried to close it.

"You and Dr. Twin both seemed to know Rosetta. What are you not telling me?"

"A lot." I told him bitterly. "Good night Noah."

"Eve."

"I will do everything I can to help Aiden."

"Fine." He let his hand drop. "Call me at the pack's number if you need anything."

Chapter Three

Noah

I cursed the morning alarm, slapping the button to silence it. I had next to no sleep. My mind had been replaying all of last night's events, from Aiden's predicament to Dr. Twin's diagnosis of both Aiden and myself. Keep my heart stimulated. That wasn't going to be a problem if I stayed near Eve. Her peachy scent had permeated my car, essentially following me home.

With a groan, I kicked off the sheets and forced myself to my feet. It was going to be a long day. Lumbering to the bathroom, I took my time in the hot shower. Thoughts of Eve had me turning the water from hot to cold. I couldn't get the image of her beautiful stormy grey eyes out of my mind, making me wonder how she became blind.

Eventually, I got dressed, made coffee then went to the office. The pack lives in a community behind a horse ranch. The ranch is a tourist attraction to bring in a small profit and provides riding lessons. Being secluded from the city, it's also a great place to run wild during a full moon and train young wolves to control their new instincts.

My office is in the community center. A center point in our community. Here pack members can come to me personally with their problems, or if they're shy, they can leave a note in a request box. It's a casual setting made to put the pack at ease. Alpha Jack, the previous Alpha, preferred to work out of his house. There were questions as to why I didn't do the same thing. My answer is simple; if you need to see me at my house, you must have an emergency.

Tate stood outside my office with his arms crossed over his muscled chest and his perpetual scowl on his face. His buzz-cut black hair and cold eyes make him look scary, and when he's pissed he's truly scary. He was Jack's Beta, and when I became Alpha, I kept him. He was loyal to Jack but even more loyal to the pack. Though he didn't like seeing Jack get replaced, he agreed it was time for a change. I should find a Beta faithful to me, but Tate knows the inner workings of the pack, and with Aiden's life on the line, I don't have the mind space to find a new Beta.

"Morning Tate."

"Alpha." His voice was deep and gravely and unimpressed. "Where were you yesterday?"

"On a personal errand. You know Aiden hasn't been well. I was trying to find someone to help cure him."

"You have a lot of work to do." He stepped aside. "Let me handle Aiden."

I shook my head. Aiden is my friend, and I won't hand him over to anyone. However, I did hand him over to Eve, who handed him over to Dr. Twin. Reluctantly I entered the office. I'd rather be out with Eve, working to save Aiden. She shut me down last night, refusing my help, but I'm sure I could convince her otherwise. I'm pretty sure she knows how or where to start tracking Rosetta. I sat behind the desk and forced my thoughts back to pack business. If I don't hear from her at some point today, I'll go back to her apartment for answers.

"Haven't I made a dent in the paperwork?"

"You've been able to clean up what Alpha Jack had neglected. Now, you must catch up on everything that has piled up since you became Alpha."

I held in a groan. "Such as?"

Tate took a stack of papers from a shelf next to the door. "Pack requests."

I let out a low whistle. "That's a lot."

"I've gone through the requests daily for the past year. Anything needing immediate attention or was simple I've already completed." He explained. "These need your attention."

"Thank you." I picked up the top request and read it. "This is just a request for a fence to be built."

"You'll need to check property lines and then organize to have it built. Plus, there's a financial aspect too."

I frowned. Before handling any of these requests, I would have to sort through them. Pushing the pile on my desk to the side, I began going through every submission and placing them in new stacks. Requests for various builds such as fences, gardens, and pools. Recommendations on how to run the horse ranch. Requests for me to solve squabbles between pack members. Finally, other tasks that I can pass along to Tate.

Out of all the requests, the more pressing ones are about the squabbles. Picking up the pile, I read the top one. Two pack members are fighting over the custody of a pet. The only way to decide is to speak to both pack members. Tate followed me out of the office.

Hours passed, and I was nearly finished with the pile of requests about squabbles when a young wolf came running up to me. He stopped, hands on his knees as he caught his breath. When he stood straight, he opened his mouth to speak, looked at Tate, then closed his mouth.

"What's wrong?" I prompted.

"There's a strange wolf at the main entrance."

"Strange how?"

"She refused to identify herself but insisted on talking to you." The young wolf explained. "The guards are on edge with her."

"Describe her."

"Petite, brown hair, wears sunglasses."

My heart picked up. "You said she's at the main entrance?"

"Yes, Alpha."

"I can handle this." Tate stepped forward.

"As Alpha, I should greet our guest." I turned, handing him the pile of requests I carried. "There's no need to trouble yourself, Tate."

Something in his steel blue gaze put my hackles up. Recognition maybe. He may know Eve. She knows Julianne and even asked if the Alpha sent me. She had to be referring to Jack. Tate must know her. After a moment, Tate lowered his head.

"As you wish, Alpha."

I turned to the young wolf, gesturing that he should lead the way. The main entrance to the pack's community is guarded to prevent tourists from wandering beyond the ranch. It's not overly protected. We don't want to draw too much attention. Today's guest, though, attracted the attention of quite a few pack members. As I neared, the crowd dispersed to let me through.

Two guards held Eve down, with a hand on each shoulder. The unforgiving gravel under her knees must be uncomfortable, yet she didn't struggle to free herself of their hold. Instead, she kept her head down submissively. The whole scene pissed me off.

"Let her go." I ordered, struggling not to growl at them.

The guards looked at me wide-eyed. With a curt nod, they stepped back. I held a hand down in her line of sight, hoping she could see at least its shape. Eve looked up at me. Those damned sunglasses blocked my view of her gorgeous stormy eyes.

"Let me help you up."

She shook her head and pushed off the ground. Part way up, Eve dusted off her jeans. I let my hand drop. I shouldn't feel rejected by her not accepting my hand. She probably didn't see it. When Eve stood straight, she looked around nervously, wrapping her arms around herself and hunching her shoulders.

"Is there somewhere we can talk?" Eve asked quietly.

"Of course."

With a hand on her back, I guided her to my house. I glanced at the onlookers. Eve is not some freak show for them to gawk at. Once at my place, I guided her to the kitchen in the back. Less likely that a pack member will see us from the front window.

"Do you want a drink? Coffee? Water?"

"Coffee would be nice." She took a seat at the kitchen table. "Two sugars."

"Coming right up."

We stayed silent while I made the coffee. I have a single-cup-style machine, so preparing the coffee didn't take long. Eve carefully placed her hands on the kitchen table and drew them together until they wrapped around the mug. I took the seat next to her, pulling it out and positioning it so I could look at her directly.

"So." I prompted. "What brings you here?"

"I tried calling."

"You did?"

Eve nodded. "A few times."

The secretary at the community center would have taken the call, but she should have passed it along to me. Now that I think about it, Tate seemed to be on the phone a few times while we were out. He must have received the messages from the secretary. He should have told me. I made a mental note to scold Tate for that later.

"Sorry." I told Eve. "I was helping various pack members."

She nodded as if she understood. "Can you tell me where Aiden met his ex?"

I took a moment to think about it. "I believe it was at a business event."

"What kind of event?"

"A meet-and-greet between various companies and clients."

"What does Aiden do?"

"By day, he's a lawyer, and by night he's our healer." I smiled at the memory of Aiden saving me from exposure as a wolf in college. "Aiden has always helped people. It's in his nature."

Eve sipped her coffee. I watched her profile. Through the side of the sunglasses, I caught a glimpse of her eyes. I didn't realize I had moved forward until it was too late to backtrack. I removed those damned sunglasses. Eve's eyes widened as she looked at me.

"What are you doing?"

"Your eyes are beautiful." I blurted out.

A blush graced her cheeks. I shifted in my seat. My wolf urged me to touch her, get closer, and claim her. I cleared my throat, a little unnerved by this woman's pull on me, yet unable to resist her.

"Last night, you and Dr. Twin mentioned someone named Heartless. Were you talking about Rosetta?"

Eve stiffened. "Yes."

"So you've crossed paths with Rosetta before?"

"Yes."

"Will you tell me what happened?"

Eve took a deep breath staring as if studying me. "Five years ago, I was tasked with bringing back a young man who was mesmerized by a beautiful woman."

"Did you bring him back?"

"No." Eve closed her eyes and shook her head. "I was too late."

I stared at Eve. Too late? As in, he passed away? Was he in a state similar to Aiden's? A tear slid down her cheek. With the pad of my thumb, I brushed it away. The skin-to-skin touch was electrifying. Eve sucked in a sharp breath and opened her eyes. She jerked back from me so quickly that my hand fell from her face. She stood quickly, the chair falling to the floor behind her. I stood, too, afraid she was going to trip.

"Eve?"

I could hear her heart pounding furiously in her chest. Eve reached for her sunglasses. Not wanting her to cover her eyes again, I reached out to stop her. Panic seemed to fill her features, she jerked her hand back, away from me, before we made contact.

"You don't need to cover your eyes when it's just us." I insisted.

Chapter Four

Eve

Noah's touch woke every nerve ending in my body. Every. Single. Nerve. The simple brush of his thumbs along my cheek had to be a fluke. Too afraid to test his touch again I avoided contact when he reached to stop me from grabbing my sunglasses. When he touched me I saw colour for the first time in five years. It scared me. Green eyes stared back at me — until I pulled away. Gray is safe.

I kicked the chair away to put some much-needed distance between us. "You said Aiden is a lawyer. Which company does he work at?"

"I can take you." Noah offered.

"No. I can take a taxi."

"Don't be ridiculous. It's a waste of money when I'm perfectly capable of taking you."

He has a point. My wolf whined, clawing at my mind, wanting to be closer to Noah. I want to get closer, to feel his warmth, and to see colour again — but I'm too scared. I've never crossed paths with anyone who can be seen in lighter shades of grey — let alone in colour. If Noah drives me around, the temptation of having him touch me so I can see colour again is too strong. Yet, it'll save me taxi fare.

"Fine." I straightened my shoulders. "You can drive, just don't touch my skin."

"I can do that."

I watched Noah's shape leave his spot and retreat. I waited before snagging my sunglasses from the table, then followed. Noah waited for me, and falling into step beside me, he placed a hand on my back. The warmth of his hand soothed my wolf but unnerved me. I should have told him not to touch me at all.

Noah helped me into his car and drove off. I kept my hands on my lap and angled away from him. The closer I am to him, the more I want to touch him. My wolf's nudging doesn't help my resolve to keep some distance. We stayed silent. Noah's scent wrapped around me in the small space — my decision to let him drive tested my resolve to maintain a professional distance.

Noah parked and came around to open the car door for me, followed by the entrance to the building. The gentlemanly acts irked me. It made me feel like I could not complete such simple actions alone. My irritation was quickly overridden when I walked into the building and smelled apples, like freshly baked apple pie. Adam's scent. But that's impossible.

I tried to back out, but Noah stood at my back. He placed his hands on my shoulders, and I could feel his concern before he spoke.

"What's wrong?

"Where are we?" I could hear the strain in my voice as I struggled to breathe.

"Lowers and Sons Law Firm."

My stomach flopped, and my breathing stopped. This is where Adam worked. His scent shouldn't be lingering in the lobby after five years. I felt my body shake slightly but wasn't registering the movement. A light spark at my arm drew my attention to Noah. He touched my skin for the briefest moment.

"Are you okay?"

I wasn't all right, but I wasn't about to tell him that. I nodded. If I spoke, I might reveal that I'm not okay in this building.

"I'm sorry I touched you." Noah apologized. "But you looked like you might have been having a panic attack, and I didn't know how else to get your attention."

I only nodded again. Noah was careful to touch only covered skin as he guided me. The distinct ding told me he'd led me to the elevators. His gentle push meant the doors were open. I gripped the safety bar for dear life.

"Eve?"

"Just tell me when to get off."

"Are you claustrophobic?"

"I'm a blind person using an elevator." I bit out bitterly.

"Oh." Noah said sheepishly. "You wouldn't be able to see what floor it's stopping at."

The soft jostle of the steel box indicated its stop, then the subtle swoosh sound of the doors opening. Noah wrapped an arm around my waist, tugging me into his chest as grey figures entered the elevator.

The small space felt cramped. The doors closed, and the metal box jerked upward. When the doors opened again, Noah urged me off with a gentle push. His hand shifted to my left and right side when he needed me to turn. I appreciated the quiet directions as he maneuvered me through all the grey forms.

"Robert." Noah stopped walking. "Do you have a few minutes?"

"Noah!" A male voice answered. "This is a surprise. What brings you here?"

"This is Eve. I've asked her to track down Aiden's ex."

"A pleasure." Robert stated.

I watched a grey form grow. Suspecting he was sitting and was now standing. I couldn't be sure if he was extending his hand in greeting like so many people tend to do. Not wanting to look foolish, I kept my hands to myself.

"Uhm. Why do you need to find Aiden's girlfriend?"

"Aiden is asking for her." I answered. "And she seems to have disappeared."

"I don't know how much help I can be."

"Have you met her before?"

"A couple of times. The first time was at the same business event where Aiden met her. She made the first move, which was pretty bold, and Aiden was enraptured."

I tried not to cringe. The memory of Adam being enraptured by this witch floated to the forefront of my mind. When she finds someone that catches her eye, she won't stop until she has him under her spell.

"I've never met her." Noah stated. "What does Rosetta look like?"

"She's a real beauty." Robert answered with longing in his voice. "Long red hair, gorgeous green eyes, porcelain skin. She'd be flawless if it weren't for the three angry red lines across her cheek. Ironically they make her appear more human."

Robert's scent changed when he spoke of the witch. It was subtle, but her magic lingered — strawberry champagne, sweet and bubbly.

"When was the last time you saw her?" I asked.

"Yesterday. She left me her contact information to give to Aiden."

"Wouldn't Aiden already have all that?"

"She changed her number."

I heard some shuffling of papers.

"You can pass it along to Aiden for me. I haven't seen him in a few days."

"He's in the hospital." Noah lied. "Got into an accident. Broken ribs, nearly puncturing his heart."

"Oh my. I hope he heals."

"The doctor is uncertain. There's much damage. But I'm hopeful." Noah put a hand on my back. "I'll be sure to pass this along to Aiden."

I was guided back to the elevators. Julianne works in this building on the same floor that Adam worked. I wanted to talk to her and ask her if she's seen him, but I decided not to, not with Noah at my side. I'll call her later. This case is bringing back too many memories of Adam. I want to know why she told Noah to come to me. Surely she knew what he needed and how it'll affect me.

"Where to next?" Noah inquired.

"Home."

"Home? Why?"

I sucked in a breath seconds before the elevator door opened. Rushing out of the elevator, I tried to determine where the exit was before I needed to get oxygen to my lungs again. Noah seemed to sense my urgency and helped me outside. I took deep breaths, choking on engine fumes lingering in the air.

"What's wrong? What is it about this building that has you on edge?"

"You ask too many questions." I accused.

"I'm curious."

"Curiosity killed the cat." I quipped dryly.

Noah's bark of laughter startled me. The deep rumble of it did something to my insides. It made me realize that I haven't heard a laugh in so long. People tend to be solemn around me. Now that I think about it, I don't think I've laughed since I lost Adam.

"It's a good thing I'm not a cat."

He'd leaned in. His voice was low and seductive. Was he flirting? My heart picked up again. It's been doing that more often when Noah's near. A need to touch him, to see his facial expression bubbled up inside. I squashed it and cleared my throat.

"Please take me home, Noah."

He pulled back. "Very well."

"Thank you." I got out of the car as quickly as possible. "I'll call you when I have something."

Noah didn't say anything. He didn't say anything the entire car ride. His pine scent was messing with my mind. I need to get away from him. I need to be focused. Rosetta will reach out. At least, I hope she does. If I'm right, then Rosetta's magic on Robert will compel him to call her about me. She'll reach out to taunt me, to retaliate in some way for the scars I left on her face.

If Rosetta reaches out, then maybe, just maybe, I can get Adam back. My hands shook as I inserted the key into my apartment door. What will I do if I get Adam back? Besides being blind, I'm not the same person I was five years ago. Would my wolf want him again? Would she react to Adam the same way she acts to Noah?

Noah's scent wrapped around me as if I'd conjured him from my thoughts. I looked over my shoulder to see his light grey form approach from the stairs. He pushed me inside, and then I heard the click of the lock being put in place.

"Go home, Noah." I ordered weakly.

"No." He stated firmly. "You're holding back."

I pursed my lips. He already knows I've run into Rosetta in the past. What more does he want from me? I stood still as Noah removed my sunglasses, careful not to touch my face. It took a lot of willpower not to tilt my head just a few centimetres so his hand would brush my cheek. Instead, I forced myself to take a step back.

"I need you to leave." My voice sounded thin and weak.

"I'm not leaving you, Eve."

Those words broke me. Adam said the same thing when he was trying to earn my trust. Then, after three years, he left me, lured in by

Rosetta's beauty and magic. I wrapped my arms around myself and blinked back the tears threatening to fall.

The sound of cupboards opening and closing drew my attention toward the kitchen. I spun to see Noah's shape in the space. Porcelain clinked, and I realized he was grabbing coffee mugs.

"I can get a pack member to run the phone number Rosetta gave Robert." Noah stated. "It could lead us right to her."

"Or it could be a wild goose chase." I told him.

"I'm willing to chase any potential lead with you."

"I work better alone."

"No one is better alone." He countered, twisting my words. "You're not getting rid of me that easily."

I moved into the small kitchen and crossed my arms. "You'll only be around until I miraculously find the witch and save Aiden."

"You're wrong." Noah whispered.

"What?"

"You're wrong." He said louder.

I sensed determination from Noah as he closed the distance between us. My wolf was restless in my mind. His scent overwhelmed my senses. The heat from his proximity had me backing up not to get burned. Noah followed my every step until a solid surface at my back stopped my retreat.

"Why are you scared of me?"

My throat closed up. Because you make me feel. I was unable to speak the words. I could feel the heat from Noah's hand near my cheek. I want to feel his warm hand against my skin. All afternoon I wanted him to touch me. I wanted to see the blue sky as he drove. I wanted to watch Robert's reactions as I questioned him. I don't deserve to see anything. Alpha Jack was right when he kicked me out of the pack. I'm useless and deserve to stay blind for losing Adam.

"I want to touch you." Noah pleaded.

I swallowed hard. If he touches me, then I'll see colour again. My gut tightened. I want to see colour again. I deserve that much after so long, don't I? Closing my eyes, I tilted my head into his palm. If wolves could purr, I'm sure mine would be. A complete sense of rightness washed over me. Noah ran his thumb just beneath my eye.

"Why won't you look at me?" He asked softly.

"I'm scared." I replied just as softly.

"Of what?"

I can't say exactly. No words would be strong enough to adequately explain my reason for being scared. Maybe it's the intimacy of touch that I'm scared of. How I need Noah to bring colour back into my life scares me. Noah's lips brush against mine. The act was shocking, forcing my eyes to open. His green eyes sparkled, and a cocky smirk was plastered on his face.

"There we go." He teased.

"Why did you do that?"

Noah shrugged. I could see his shoulders move up and down. Strong shoulders, encased in a white t-shirt, moved. Noah's thumb brushed my cheek, and leaned forward to place his forehead against mine. His lips were so close. All I had to do was tilt my head back, and he could kiss me again. I felt giddy with the thought of his lips on mine.

"I wanted you to open your eyes." He stated. "And because I wanted to know if you'd let me kiss you."

I started to tilt my head back when a beeping drew my attention to somewhere beyond Noah's shoulder. The coffee machine was signalling its completion. I saw the full pot of coffee and two mismatched mugs on the counter waiting to be filled. Noah sighed, then stepped back, his hand dropping from my cheek. I scrambled to grab his hand, not wanting to lose this colourful world that quickly. Noah looked back at me, but I was focused on my apartment. My very dark apartment.

"I really let this place go."

Chapter Five

Noah

I stared at Eve, but she wasn't looking at me. She was looking beyond me. At her apartment.

"The coffee is ready." I stated stupidly.

She nodded, walking with me back to the kitchen. I tried taking my hand back, but she squeezed it tighter as if afraid to let go. Using my non-dominant hand, I poured the coffee into mugs. Eve switched hands and walked down the short length of cabinets to open a door. Picking up my coffee, I watched her take out a plate from the upper cabinets and scowled at it.

Putting it down, she then walked over to the fridge. Opening the door, she bent forward. I shifted to get a better view of her ass. My wolf growled his appreciation. Eve handed me a jar of queso gone green. I put my coffee down to take it.

"Toss this in the garbage." She reached in and handed me a jar of mouldy salsa. "And this."

I put the queso down to take the salsa. "What is happening?"

Eve ignored me. Closing the fridge, she caught sight of the calendar, skimming her fingers along the dates. Her shoulders dropped, and I felt her sadness. The calendar was for February, dated five years ago. She looked lost in thought.

"Eve?"

She jumped, started by my voice and turned to me. Her grey eyes were lighter, and I could see a hint of colour beneath. She tried to pull her hand back, but I entwined our fingers, refusing to let her go.

"Can you see?"

She nodded.

"How?"

"I don't know." She admitted softly, her gaze falling to our hands. "But when you touch me, I see colour again."

I took in a sharp breath. I wanted to tell her never to let go but somehow knew that would scare her off. Instead, I remained silent. This connection between us is more than either one of us anticipated. Since becoming Alpha, I stopped looking for a mate, but fate found her for me. My wolf howled in my head. My mate. Eve looked back at the calendar, and my heart tightened. She must not have moved on from someone in her past, and if I push too hard, she may retreat from a future with me.

"Your coffee has gotten cold."

"Thanks." She mumbled.

Eve picked up a mug from the counter and freed her hand from mine. My wolf whined at the loss of contact. I watch as her eyes turn stormy again. Had she held on longer, would I have been able to see what colour her eyes used to be? Her nose scrunched up after a sip.

"Want me to pour a fresh cup?"

Eve shook her head. "Needs sugar."

I couldn't help but laugh. "Two sugars coming right up."

I opened the cupboard where I found the ground coffee and pulled out two sugar packets. Opening them, I then poured their contents into her mug. I searched for a spoon to stir it in, then deemed the coffee drinkable. Eve took a sip and nodded her approval.

"About that phone number." I brought up a semi-safe topic, needing to fill the silence between us.

"You can do whatever you want." Eve's tone turned bitter. "It won't lead you anywhere."

"How would you know?"

"I could smell the witch's magic on Robert. A spell she would have woven so he'd call her if anyone started asking questions."

"What do you suggest?"

"Wait."

"Wait?" I repeated, dumbfounded by her answer. "For how long? Aiden doesn't have much time."

"A day, maybe two. Dr. Twin's magic would be blocking the witch from finding Aiden. She'll want to reach out to get him to her side."

"I'm not going to sit around and do nothing."

Eve scowled, shoving the coffee mug at me. "You asked for my help. If you don't want it, get out and do things your way."

I grabbed the bottom of the mug seconds before she let go. Eve then turned and stormed off. The slamming of a door was a telltale sign that she was pissed. With a sigh, I turned to the sink to wash the mugs. Needing to stay busy, I washed all her dishes. There was dried food on some pieces. Perfectly understandable if she can't see the cheese stuck between the fork prongs or the egg yolk stubbornly attached to the plate. For the most part, the dishes are clean.

I mulled over Eve's behaviour as I washed the dishes. She's far too emotional about this whole Rosetta situation. It made me wonder if she had a connection to the man she spoke of earlier, the one who was mesmerized by a beautiful woman. The one she lost. Is the guilt of not saving him eating away at her? Or is there another reason she quickly decided to help me save Aiden?

There's nothing I can do but wonder about Eve and her past. Despite her belief that the phone number provided won't help, I have to try anyway. I pulled out the phone number from my pocket, along with my phone, and called a pack member who works on the police force.

"Gordon."

"Noah." Gordon replied in hushed tones. "I mean Alpha Noah."

"No need for the Alpha in front of my name." I've never really understood why Jack insisted everyone call him Alpha Jack.

"Yes, sorry." He cleared his throat. "Why are you calling me?"

"I need you to trace a number for me."

"That would be a misuse of police resources."

"It's for Aiden." I explained. "He's in trouble, and I think this number will help me to help him."

Gordon hesitated. "Very well. What's the number?"

I rattled the ten digits off to him. Typing could be heard on the other end of the line as I waited impatiently for an answer. Soft sobs caught my attention. I moved down the short hall to the closed door. Silently turning the knob, I cracked the door open. Eve's sorrow hit me hard, like it was my sorrow. I wanted to fling the door open and hold her in my arms.

"Adam." Eve sobbed.

I froze. Who is Adam? I gripped the doorknob tightly. I wanted to comfort her, but another man's name on her lips stopped me cold. My wolf growled its dislike of this Adam person.

"That's unfortunate." Gordon grumbled.

I closed the door, retreating to the living room. "What?"

"The phone is offline. It was last used on Prastin Street earlier today, but I can't seem to turn it back on. The SIM card must have been pulled."

"Thanks, Gordon."

"Sorry, I can't do more."

"You've done plenty."

I hung up and sank on the couch. Prastin Street is a lead. I itched to see what I could find out, but Eve's soft sobs glued me to my seat. I can't leave her vulnerable. I'll go in the morning. Eve won't want to go and probably insist it'll be a waste of time, but I want to ensure she's okay before I leave.

My body ached from an uncomfortable sleep. The scent of peaches permeated my senses. That scent stirred the need of both the man and the wolf. Sitting up, I looked around Eve's apartment. She was nowhere to be seen, but at some point in the night, she must have left her room to put a blanket over me, which is now on the floor. How did I not realize she was right here?

Getting up, I went to check on Eve. I knocked gently and then carefully opened the bedroom door. She was still asleep. I decided I'd have time to run out and grab us breakfast before she fully wakes up. I snatched her keys from the entryway table where she had dropped them last night. If I recall correctly, there's a café down the street.

The place was busy. I waited in line. Reaching the front, I ordered two coffees, two breakfast wraps, and two muffins. I paid for the order and then moved to the end of the counter to wait. The team behind the counter worked efficiently to fulfill the orders flying in.

I collected my order and then returned to Eve. My growling wolf warned me something wasn't right. Eve's apartment door was unlocked, and I know I locked it before leaving. It was hard to tell if Eve was even there since the whole place smelled like her. But there was another scent, too, subtle and barely noticeable.

"Eve?" I called out cautiously.

No answer. I went to the kitchen to put to coffee and breakfast down. My ears were primed for any little sound. Nothing. I went down the short hall to her bedroom only to find it empty. Fear gripped me. I didn't see a note. She had to realize I had taken her keys and would be coming back. That strange scent was more potent in her room. Was Eve kidnapped?

I froze in the doorway to the hall, about to leave to track her down, when Eve backed out of the apartment across the hall. I gripped the doorframe to stop myself from sagging to the floor with relief. An elderly woman followed her to the door.

"Thank you so much for your help, dear."

"It was my pleasure, Mrs. Zaw." Eve replied.

"I can't imagine what would have scared Snuffles that badly." The woman held a Pomeranian close to her chest. "He's usually so tough."

"Maybe it was just a bad dream." Eve leaned in to pet the puffball. "We all get them from time to time."

"I find it hard to imagine you having bad dreams with such a strong man beside you."

Eve's shoulders stiffened. "Strong man?"

The elderly woman clicked her tongue. "The one in your apartment."

The woman waggled her fingers at me. I raised a hand in greeting. Eve turned, a frown on her lips. She wore her sunglasses, but I could easily picture her glaring. Mrs. Zaw shut the door to her apartment.

I stepped back for Eve to enter her apartment. Shutting and locking the door, I followed Eve into the kitchen. She tossed her sunglasses onto the counter and then turned to me with her hands on her hips. Her stormy eyes seemed to darken as she narrowed a glare at me. I couldn't help but grin. She looked cute. My eyes roamed over her body, barely covered by shorts and a tank top. No, not cute. Eve is the sexiest woman I've ever seen. I itched to touch her, to run my hands over her curves, and haul her against my body. I bet she'd fit perfectly.

"I thought you left." She stated.

"Taking your keys with me?" I shook my head, even if she couldn't see it. "You can't get rid of me that easily."

"Where did you go?"

"To get us breakfast."

Eve's gaze widened in surprise. "Oh."

"I have coffee, breakfast wraps, and for dessert — muffins."

Eve didn't say anything. Careful not to touch her skin, I gripped Eve by the hips and lifted her onto the counter. She grabbed my shoulders with a little squeak. I ordered her to put out her hands and then placed the wrap in them. She unwrapped it and began eating. I placed her coffee next to her leg so she could feel the heat of it and know where it was.

"Muffins aren't dessert." Eve finally said.

"Not even double chocolate?"

I watched her lips purse as she debated the answer. Taking my wrap, I began to eat, leaning against the counter next to her. I'd rather stand between her legs kissing her, but Eve has been trying to resist our connection. Maybe when Aiden is saved, I can pursue her without abandon.

"Did you get double chocolate?" Eve asked quietly.

"I did."

"I still wouldn't call a muffin dessert."

I chuckled. Eve fell silent again, eating her breakfast and sipping the coffee. When she finished, I handed her the muffin at her request. She took a bite and groaned. The sound filled with such pleasure almost had me groaning with painful need.

"What are your plans for today?" I needed to break the silence.

"A potential client reached out last night." Eve stated, her body tensing. "I'll take the meeting, then get back to looking for the witch."

"I'll come with you."

"No." Her nose wrinkled. "Go home. Shower, change."

I couldn't argue the need for a change of clothes. "Fine, but I'm coming right back."

Chapter Six

Eve

I lied to Noah about meeting a potential client only because I needed him out of my apartment. When I woke up this morning, my bedroom smelt of apples and strawberry champagne. Somehow Adam and that witch, or maybe it was just one of them, entered my room without me or Noah noticing. I needed Noah gone to figure out why those scents were lingering.

Locking the door behind Noah, I returned to my bedroom. A ringing phone came from somewhere in this room. And it's not mine. I ran my hands over the duvet until my fingers touched a cold rectangular shape. I picked up the small vibrating, and ringing device, flipped it open and hoped the button I pushed answered it.

I put the phone to my ear. "Hello?"

"Eve." A sickeningly sweet voice elongated my name with a hint of reminiscence in her tone. "It's so good to hear from you."

"Too bad I can't relay the feeling." I bit out.

"So rude." She tsked playfully.

"Get to your point, witch."

Rosetta took a breath, her tone turning cold. "You have my warlock."

"Do I?" I teased mockingly, proud she hadn't found Aiden yet. "I didn't see your name on him."

"I want him back. Tonight."

"I can't do that."

"Sure you can." Rosetta's chipper tone returned. "We can make a trade. My warlock for your wolf."

I took in a sharp breath. I can get Adam back. The trade is tempting.

"I'll text over the address." Rosetta proclaimed. "You have until midnight Eve."

The witch hung up on me. It took me a minute to pull the phone away. Can I genuinely trade Aiden for Adam? In a sense, be betraying Noah. This is all too much. I need to talk to Julianne. She can help me sort through everything.

"This is Julianne." She responded cheerfully when I dialled her number from memory.

"Julianne, it's Eve."

"Eve. How are you? Is everything okay?"

"No, everything is not okay." I felt my throat start to close up.

"Talk to me." Julianne ordered.

"Why did you send Noah my way?"

She didn't answer immediately.

"Julianne." I groaned. "Did you know what his situation was?"

"Not fully." She admitted. "I knew Aiden was in trouble, and Noah would do anything for his friend. I knew that whatever the situation, you could help."

"Aiden lost his heart to Heartless."

"Oh." There was regret in her tone. "I'm sorry, Eve."

"She reached out. Willing to trade Aiden for Adam."

"Don't." Julianne stated firmly. "You can't seriously think that witch will give you Adam back without some sort of catch?"

"If I don't give her Aiden, then he could die. I don't know how to save him." Tears began to choke me. "And I could have Adam back. I could redeem myself."

"Have you talked to Noah?"

I shook my head. "No."

Julianne took a deep breath. "Noah would know what's best. Talk to him."

"I'm scared."

"Of Noah? Why? He's a perfectly nice guy. He's kind and thoughtful and can't forget good-looking."

"I can see with him." I blurted.

There was a beat of silence. "Repeat that."

"I can see with Noah. When he touches my skin, I see colour again."

"I'm not sure how to take that." Julianne admitted. "Should I be happy? Or should I be scared?"

"I don't know."

We both fell silent. I wished she was here with me. I wanted to feel comforted by her arms, telling me everything would be all right. It's all too much. My best friend is supposed to help me sort through my problems, not be just as confused about them as I am.

Finally, Julianne spoke. "How do you feel about Noah?"

"What do you mean?"

"Do you like him? Does he frighten you?"

I nibbled my thumbnail, contemplating. "I like him, I guess. My wolf seems to like him."

"Your wolf?" She repeated, surprised. "She woke up?"

48

I nodded, even if she couldn't see it. "The moment I opened the door when he came to me with Aiden's problem."

"That's a good thing, Eve."

"I don't want to like Noah. He's only going to be around long enough to save Aiden. Once that's done, he's just going to abandon me."

"Has Noah shown any signs of wanting to leave you after you help Aiden?"

I thought about it. His kisses seemed needy. His words from last night seemed honest. Can I trust those? Adam was the same way. Except, with Adam, my wolf wasn't as eager to be close to him compared to Noah.

"No, but neither did Adam."

"If you want my opinion."

"I do." I cut her off.

"Then I think you should give Noah a chance. You can't stay lost in the past forever. You have to move on from Adam. And you can't let Adam's abandonment stop you from trying to find your mate." Julianne told me. "And this whole trade Aiden for Adam thing, I don't think you should do it. I think that witch is tricking you. She'd never give you Adam. I also think you should talk it over with Noah."

I mumbled thanks and hung up on Julianne. That conversation could have been more helpful. I went for a shower and changed my clothes. I thought it over and made my decision. I have to try and get Adam back. Even if it is a trick. I have to try to redeem myself. Alpha Jack will be so happy if I can bring Adam back to him. Grabbing the flip phone, I left my apartment.

Will welcomed me when I entered Dr. Twin's office. The building is open during the day for walk-in clients. Only at night do they use codes to identify who wants entry. I've been told it's because the worst always happens at night. I have no idea what it means, Dr. Twin is a strange warlock, but he's good at what he does. Upon my request, Will helped me to Aiden's room. I stared at the grey form, Rosetta's trade still echoing in my mind.

"Darling, what are you doing here?" Dr. Twin's voice came from behind me.

"Contemplating how to execute my next move."

"Do tell."

"Heartless reached out, offering me a trade. Aiden for Adam."

"Absolutely not."

Dr. Twin's magic flared with his anger. The heat of it licked my skin before he reigned it in. I've never been able to see him use magic, but I've always imagined it looking like a rainbow. Bright and colourful, just like him.

"You can't hand Aiden over to that witch." He put a hand on my shoulder.

"That's what Julianne said."

"She's a smart woman, that friend of yours."

"I want to bring Adam back. I have to."

"I know, Darling."

Dr. Twin turned me around gently and wrapped me in his arms. His hug was comforting. Dr. Twin has been with me every day since Rosetta took my sight. He helped me adjust to the new grey world. He's also the only one who knows exactly what happened to Adam. Julianne knows that Rosetta lured Adam in with magic and that he chose to stay with her. She doesn't know that I knelt in from of him and he couldn't see me. His so-called love for me wasn't strong enough to break Rosetta's spell.

With a resigned sigh, I leaned into Dr. Twin. "I don't want to give Heartless what she wants."

"Then don't."

"Giving her Aiden may be the only way to save him."

"Maybe not." He kissed the top of my head. "Wait right here."

Dr. Twin left me in the room with Aiden. I turned back to Aiden, walking closer until I bumped into him. Or rather, bumped into the chair I know he's restrained in. Being in this room with him, I began to waver on my earlier decision. How could I even consider trading Aiden for Adam? It's been five years. There's no way Adam would be the same person even if I were to release him from Rosetta's magic. No, I won't give Aiden to her. I won't let her take another victim. There has to be another way to save him.

"Rosetta." Aiden gargled.

I heard him struggling against his restraints and touched him. "She's not here."

"Save me."

"From her?" I questioned hopefully.

"Yes." He hissed out.

I squeezed what I hoped was his leg. "I'll do my best."

Aside from killing the witch, I'm unsure how to save Aiden. Her midnight deadline will come faster than anticipated, and I need a plan before then.

"Okay." Dr. Twin returned. "I called in a favour. There will be a car waiting for you out back."

"Excuse me?" I turned to him, confused.

"I will transfer a portion of Aiden's soul into a dummy. You'll need to be in constant contact with the dummy. The moment you let go, his soul will return here."

"I don't understand."

"Darling, if you're going to save Aiden, you must get close to Heartless."

Now I understood. Pretend to give the witch what she wants, get close enough to figure out how to save Aiden, then run like hell away from her. Dr. Twin gently moved me and then clapped his hands together. I couldn't see him work his magic, but I could feel it. Its warmth swirled around the room. Tendrils of magic wrapped around my wrist, guiding me to take hold of something firm.

"Remember not to let go." Dr. Twin reminded me. "Your ride should be here now."

"Thank you."

"Don't. I'm calling Noah as soon as you leave."

I scowled at him. If Noah catches up, he will stop me. I tightened my hold on the dummy. It followed me out the back door and down the steps. The dummy moved surprisingly well. With a hand on the railing to keep myself from falling, what felt like uneven metal stairs, I found it challenging to keep my balance since my free hand had to stay plastered to the dummy. Just as Dr. Twin stated, I could hear the sound of a car engine running at the bottom of the stairs.

"You must be Eve." A rough voice snickered. "The good doctor used a favour on you. You must be very special for him to do that."

"And you are?"

"Where am I taking you?"

He ignored my question and helped me into the car. I handed him the flip phone, which should contain an address.

The man gave a low whistle. "That's out of town."

Aside from that comment, he made no complaint about driving me. The car smelt overwhelmingly of cigar smoke. The scent covered the man, masking whatever supernatural creature he may be. He closed my door, moments later entered the car and drove away.

"Dang." Cigar man let out an appreciative sound. "This house is huge."

"You can leave me here." I told him.

"You sure?"

"Yes. Though if you could go to the tourist horse ranch and tell someone by the name of Noah where I am, it would be appreciated. If you tell him Aiden is here, he'll surely come."

He seemed to ponder my request. "Very well, but I will come to collect payment for this request later."

I couldn't help but smile. "I'll start a tab."

His chuckle rumbled huskily with years of cigar use. I tugged the dummy gently out of the car and stood outside as the vehicle drove away. I thought about it all the way here, and I should have told Dr. Twin where I was going so he could tell Noah. I'd feel more confident facing Rosetta with Noah by my side.

Rosetta's strawberry champagne magic permeated the area. I couldn't even smell any flowers or grass if there was any. Completely stranded and blind is a horrible combination. My wolf shrank back, her fear doubling my fear.

"Eve!" Rosetta called out gleefully. "You came."

I turned to her voice. "How is Adam?"

"Come inside, have some tea."

I hesitated. A hand was placed on my back, urging me forward. I felt Rosetta's magic swirl around my limbs, helping me move. My grip tightened on the dummy, afraid I'd let go too soon. Rosetta led the way in her home. The room she led me to held four other grey figures. Hands forced me down onto a couch.

"I'm thrilled you brought Aiden." Rosetta cooed.

"Reluctantly." I admitted.

"A deal is a deal. Now, hand Aiden over."

"I don't trust you to hold up your end."

With a dramatic sigh, something happened. I could hear movement. See one of the figures move to stand next to where I saw her sit down. I felt her magic expand in the room, then suddenly it snapped back.

"Eve?"

I sucked in a breath. "Adam?"

"What are you doing here?"

"Now, Aiden." Rosetta ordered softly.

I stood. Too absorbed in the sound of Adam's voice. Unconsciously I moved forward, letting go of the dummy. My shins hit a low table, and I cursed, realizing what I'd done. I'd sent Aiden's soul back to his body. Rosetta's screech indicated she realized she'd been tricked.

"That was stupid of you, Eve."

Rosetta's magic infiltrated my mind. My grey vision darkened to nothingness. Now I really wish I'd told Dr. Twin where I was going. Noah's name was my last thought before I lost consciousness.

Chapter Seven

Noah

I went home to shower and change but didn't return to Eve immediately. Tate caught me before I had a chance to leave again. There were financial reports I had to review. After that, I went to Prastin Street. Eve refused to follow whatever lead the phone number would provide, but I could not ignore it. I'll do anything for Aiden.

I parked on Prastin Street and got out. Gordon wasn't able to narrow down an exact address, but I'd hope to be able to talk to neighbours about Aiden's red-headed ex. Kids played in a nearby park, and families were out walking their dogs. The yards looked meticulous in this quaint neighbourhood. Quiet and safe looking, it's all an illusion. I started walking down Prastin Street, hoping for a clue to tell me which house was Rosetta's.

Scents were everywhere — freshly cut grass, paint, flowers, peaches, nothing. I stopped. That can't be right. The house with flower boxes under the windows, a meticulous lawn, and a white picket fence displayed no scent besides peaches on the sidewalk. Eve must have been here. Why would she be here?

"Are you lost?"

I turned to a couple walking a small dog. "No, I'm just reminiscing."

"Oh?" The man asked suspiciously.

"A friend of mine used to live here years ago." I lied.

"Has it been long since you've seen your friend?" The woman asked.

"It has. Do you happen to know who lives here now?"

"No one. Five years ago, the elderly woman who lived here passed, I think." She turned to the man next to her, who nodded his agreement. "We only moved to the neighbourhood three years ago. That's the story we got from others in the area."

"I'm surprised the bank hasn't taken the house." I commented lightly.

"I've seen a pretty redhead stop by to maintain the yard. From what neighbours have said, she is the granddaughter of the woman who passed."

I thanked the couple, sidestepping toward the house to let them pass. The redhead they spoke of must be Rosetta. As I turned back to look at the home, I placed a hand on the fence, and magic sizzled through my body. A barrier must have surrounded the property because all the everyday scents hit me like a freight train. Including Aiden's. Then the house blew up.

The heat wave from the explosion threw me on my ass. Disoriented, I stared at the house. What the hell happened? The house was on fire. Neighbours rushed outside. Their voices mingled into one loud buzz. Someone helped me to my feet. The only lead I could scrounge up just blew up in my face. I could hear the wail of sirens in the distance.

"Hello?" I answered my ringing phone blindly, too transfixed with the burning house.

"Noah, it's Dr. Twin."

I straightened, far more attentive. "Is Aiden getting worse?"

"Not exactly." Dr. Twin hesitated. "Eve is doing something stupid."

"I'm on my way to your office."

I stumbled back to my car. A few people protested that I should get looked at by paramedics, but I ignored them. I drove off Prastin Street just as the fire trucks arrived. Followed closely by police.

The doorkeeper — Will, if I recall correctly — let me into the office. I rushed up the stairs straight to Aiden's room. I was relieved to see my friend still strapped to the chair. At least Eve didn't take Aiden to Rosetta. Dr. Twin walked in, a sense of nervousness coating his scent.

"You said Eve is doing something stupid." I started.

"Yes. Heartless reached out to her."

"When?"

"She offered a deal. Aiden for —." Dr. Twin paused.

"For who?" I gripped his shoulders and shook him lightly. "Aiden for who?"

"The one she lost five years ago."

I felt the blood drain from my face. I remember Eve's pain and guilt when she briefly told me how she knew Rosetta. She wouldn't just give someone over to Rosetta. She must have a plan.

"Aiden is still here."

Dr. Twin nodded. "His body is, but his soul is in a dummy. Or at least part of his soul. When Eve lets go of the dummy, Aiden's soul will return."

"Where did she go?" I tightened my grip on Dr. Twin. "She shouldn't be doing this alone. You should have stopped her."

"This is personal, and it's something Eve has to do. As for where she went, I have no idea."

Eve just wandered into danger with no one knowing where she went. I stumbled back into a chair. What if I lose both Aiden and Eve? If I had her number, I could have Gordon trace it. I looked up at Dr. Twin. Maybe he has it.

I couldn't track Eve. Her scent went as far as the back alley, where she got into a vehicle and disappeared. I had Gordon trace the number Dr. Twin gave me, or rather I forced him to provide it, but Eve left her phone at home.

There was nothing I could do.

I returned home. Getting out of the car, I slammed the door shut and kicked the tire. I hate this. Hate feeling useless. I hate that Eve didn't tell me where she was going. Why would she? She has no obligation to tell me her every move.

Looking up at the sky, I let out a guttural frustrated sound. My wolf howling within me. I need to do something.

"Bad day?"

I turned to the rough voice. With a cigar in his hand, a pudgy man smirked at me. I don't recognize him.

"Who are you?" I demand.

"I'm looking for Noah." He answered, ignoring my question.

"Why?"

"I have a message from Eve."

In two quick strides, I stood in front of this strange man. The top of his head hit me mid-chest. I gripped him by the shirt and slammed him into my car, lifting him off the ground so we were at eye level. There was a subtle tingle of magic on him, but it didn't feel like Aiden's magic.

"Where is she?"

I slammed him against the car for emphasis. My wolf pushed to the surface. The man casually brought the cigar to his lips and let out a puff of smoke. My nose cringed at the horrid smell, and my wolf backed down.

"Put me down, Alpha, and I'll tell you where to find Eve and Aiden."

I leaned in, growling. "Where?"

"Down, boy." He patted my hand. "Then I'll talk."

I put him down on the ground. The man didn't speak. Slowly I uncurled my fingers from his shirt.

"Where are they?" The cigar man fished something out of his pocket and held it up. "This is the address. I suggest you hurry. I left the poor girl there just over an hour ago."

I snatched the paper he held out. "Why didn't you wait for her?"

"The favour was to take her to her destination." The man took another puff of the cigar. "Then she used a favour to pass a message to you."

I stepped back. There was something about this man. I can feel it now that I've gotten some answers and have calmed down. This cigar man is powerful and dangerous. I wish I knew what he was.

"Go." He said. "Save her."

I opened the paper to see the address. It's out of town. It'll take time to get there. I can only hope Eve is okay when I arrive.

I drove up the long driveway and stared at a massive Victorian-style house. I stopped my car just at the edge of the driveway before it opened into a wide circular drive directly in front of the house. I came here with no plan and no backup.

I sent a quick text to my beta about my location before leaving the phone in the car. This place is massive. I have no idea where to start looking. Getting out of my car, I had to plug my nose. An overwhelming strawberry scent hit me. Slowly I removed my hand and took short breaths, not to get dizzy from the lack of air and that scent.

"Step one: find Eve." I told myself. "Step two: get out."

I heard a splash. Keeping a distance from the house, I wandered around the back. At least a dozen men stood around a pool area. A redhead popped out from the water. She brushed her hair from her face before climbing out of the pool. Her shapely body transfixed me. One of the men stepped forward to dry her off.

My wolf growled at me. He was warning me of danger. Taking the warning to heart, I looked away from the redhead who now lounged in the sun because my wolf's instincts have never failed me. She has to be Rosetta, just as Robert described.

With that much security out back, the house must be empty. I snuck toward the front door and got a whiff of a subtle peach scent. Eve's scent. Both my wolf and I honed in on the smell. It led us to an empty living room, or maybe it's called a sitting room in a house this large. Next, I followed it to a door toward the back of the house.

I could see the pool from where I stood. As I opened the door and slipped inside, I kept an eye out to ensure no one outside saw me. I closed the door and turned. A set of stairs led down to where Eve's peach scent came from.

My heart pounded, afraid of what I might find. I didn't dare turn on the light switch in case someone noticed the light from under the door. With a hand on the wall, I descended the darkened stairs. At the second to last step, I froze. Eve lay unconscious on the hard cement floor.

I rushed forward. Barely noticing the cobweb feeling at the bottom that I'd walked through. All my attention was on Eve. Lowering myself to the ground, I lifted her head to my lap.

"Eve." I tapped her cheek. "Eve, wake up."

She wasn't responding. There were no visible injuries. Panic rose as I called her name more frantically. She can't be dead. The subtle rise and fall of her chest told me that much.

"Come on, Eve. Wake up."

I kissed her. It won't wake her, but it settled something within me. When I pulled back, Eve let out a soft groan. Startled but relieved to hear anything pass those lips of hers, Eve sucked in a deep breath, her eyes opening wide as she sat up. Cupping her face, I kissed her again.

Eve wrapped her hand around my wrists and pulled back. "Noah? Is it really you?"

I rested my forehead against hers. "Yeah, it's me."

"What are you doing here?"

"I came to save you."

"You shouldn't have come. The witch is too dangerous." She pulled away, breaking our contact. "Adam. I have to find Adam."

Is Adam the one she lost five years ago? It didn't matter. Eve stood slowly and looked around the room. I wanted to take her hand and run, or better yet, throw her over my shoulder and leave this place behind. Eve would fight me every step. In a short time, I've realized how stubborn she can be. Plus, she might hate me if I don't help her find this Adam person.

Eve called out for Adam. A rough voice called back. She rushed to an adjoining room. I followed, not wanting her to leave my sight. This room held shelves of strangely filled jars, herbs hung from the ceiling, and a spell book lay open next to a bubbling cauldron near a brown-haired man tied to a chair.

"Adam?"

"Eve?" The man looked at her with love in his brown eyes and a bit of surprise in his face. "You need to run. Get away from here."

"Not without you."

"Leave me."

"Never." She ran her hand along his arm and found the rope binding him.

"Eve."

"No!"

"Let me help." I crouched down,

Eve shifted, giving me more space. She struggled with the knots. I'd freed both legs by the time she released his one wrist. Adam watched me as I worked.

"Who are you?" He asked.

"No one important." Eve answered.

The final rope fell, and I stared at Eve. "Seriously?"

"Thank you." Adam stood and pulled Eve into his arms. "Let's get out of here."

Eve visibly relaxed in Adam's arms. "Home."

I think my heart broke — literally. I swear I heard it crack. Felt it even. I gripped my chest, falling forward on my hands in pain, finding breathing difficult. Aiden's spell came to mind. He did say I'd understand heartbreak, and Dr. Twin did warn me to keep my heart stimulated. I was doing so well until Eve found comfort in another man's arms.

"What a touching scene."

I looked up to see Rosetta. The redhead with three scratches on her cheek stared at me with sparkling green eyes. Beautiful eyes. I felt warmth wrap around me, helping me to my feet. In the corner of my eye, I saw Adam shift Eve behind him as if to shield her.

"Young love has been reunited." Rosetta smiled, her gaze trained on me. "Yet heartbreak has taken such a strong wolf down."

"I'm not down." I growled.

"Excellent." She held out a hand. "Stay with me, and you'll never feel heartbreak again."

Her sweet strawberry scent wrapped around me. It invaded my senses, fogging my mind. I felt my wolf struggle against the fog, but it was useless, and soon I couldn't feel my wolf at all. With Rosetta, I won't have to worry about Aiden's spell on my heart. She'll protect it.

Someone took hold of my arm. I pulled it free. The tug on my arm was more insistent, forcing me to stumble and turn to the person. As I turned, soft lips pressed onto mine urgently. My wolf came charging forward. The scent of strawberries faded, being replaced by peaches.

Eve. I wrapped my arms around her and kissed her back. She never initiated a kiss before, and I would take full advantage. She tapped my shoulder. I ignored it. She pushed at it. I didn't want to put any space between us, but reluctantly let her lips go.

"Are you back?" She inquired.

My brows furrowed. "Back from where?"

"That witch almost had you under her spell."

"I can't hold this door much longer." Adam shouted at us.

Eve pushed out of my arms to join him. The two of them put all their weight against the door. Banging from the other side indicated Rosetta was trying to get in. I turned back to the room, eyes scanning for another way out. There was a bare space of brick wall between two bookshelves. Odd. I went over to it, running my hands over the bricks.

"What happened?"

"Rosetta manipulates the hearts of men." Adam answered.

"I know that much."

"Can we talk later?" Eve grumbled.

My hands pushed a loose brick, and the bare wall opened. "This way."

Adam took Eve's hand and pulled her toward me. The door burst open. Rosetta looked furious. I shut the door behind Adam and Eve. We didn't have much time. I can only hope there's an exit. Adam ran down the hall of shelves to a ladder. He took the lead, followed by Eve, and lastly, by me. I helped Eve climb, suspecting it would be difficult in the dark space we found ourselves in. I gripped her ankle. The skin-on-skin contact would let her see the rungs and help her climb up. The exit opened up to the forest that surrounds Rosetta's property.

"My car is parked at the edge of the driveway." I told them.

This time I took the lead. When Adam and I reached the car, Eve wasn't with us. I looked back at where we came from but couldn't see her.

"Where's Eve?" Adam looked around for her.

"That's what I was going to ask."

"You don't think she went back?"

"Why would she do that?"

"Those glass jars." Adam explained. "Each one contains the heart's soul of every man in her control."

I looked back at the house. Fear gripped me. Eve shouldn't have returned alone. We could have made a plan if she told me about the jars. Tires screeching had me turning back to the driveway. Tate, and other pack members, were pulling in and hopping out of vehicles.

"Alpha!" Tate boomed furiously.

"Good, you're here."

He stopped abruptly. "Adam, is that you?"

"Yeah. Wow, Tate, you look good." Adam grinned sheepishly.

"Where have you been for five years?"

"Here." He gestured to the house.

"Catch up later." I ordered. "I have to go back for Eve."

Tate scowled. "Leave her."

"No. Tate, go through the front with the pack and draw all attention your way. Don't kill anyone. All the men inside are victims of a witch. I'm backtracking and getting Eve out of this place."

Tate and I glared at each other. With a growl, he signalled the pack members to follow. I returned to the hidden entrance in the forest. Adam followed. Back down in the hall, I ordered him to start breaking the jars. I continued to the basement where I first found Eve and where blasting sounds came from. Eve's scream put a little fire in my steps.

Rushing into the open basement room, I halted at the sight. Rosetta's magic focused on Eve, crushing her into the foundation wall. My wolf took over with a growl as I lunged at the witch. Her magic dropped. For harming Eve, this witch won't leave this room alive. Taking her head in my hands, I slammed it against the floor until she no longer struggled beneath me.

Getting up, I turned to Eve. She sat slumped on the floor. "Eve!"

Chapter Eight

Eve

Darkness, as I've never experienced before, surrounded me. It didn't matter if I opened my eyes or closed them. The darkness was the same. The weight of the darkness pressed down on me. I couldn't free myself. I have no idea where I am.

"I could save you." A soft, sweet voice said.

I've heard that voice before. But from where?

"Let me save you."

Rosetta. That was Rosetta's voice. She could save me. I do not doubt that. She is powerful.

"Eve."

I couldn't do it. I can't do it. If I accept Rosetta's help from this darkness, she'll want something in return. I have nothing to give. She's already taken everything from me. I'd rather stay here in the darkness.

"Eve." The voice that called me this time had a low timber. "Eve, wake up."

There was light tapping on my cheek. Who is that? The voice is so familiar. He called my name again. It's not Adam's voice.

"Come on, Eve. Wake up."

Lips pressed against mine. My body hummed with awareness. The darkness washed away, and I could see again. Light filled me inside, and Rosetta's presence in my mind vanished. I groaned, the light too bright right after the darkness. I sucked in a breath. I sat up, eyes widening at the person who pulled me from the darkness. He cupped my cheeks and kissed me again.

I took hold of his wrists and pulled back. Green eyes stared back at me with concern. There was something hazy lingering over his head.

"Noah?" I questioned. "Is it really you?"

He rested his forehead on mine. "Yeah, it's me."

He came for me. I couldn't help the little jump my heart made. But I was more concerned for him. That hazy thing lowered onto his head and covered his ears when I spoke.

"Thank you for coming."

"I came to save you." He responded.

"I figured that. We should get out of here before that witch returns." I pulled back, breaking contact and plunging into the familiar grey world. "I wonder if Adam is still free."

I stood from Noah's lap and looked around the solid grey room. On a whim, I called out for Adam. It was rough, but Adam called back. Rosetta must not have put him back under her spell. I rushed toward the voice, lowering my eyes so I wouldn't bump into any object. The path to Adam was clear of obstacles.

"Adam?"

There are too many things in this new room for me to distinguish exactly where he is. The scent of magic permeated the space. It must be where Rosetta performs her potions.

"Eve?" Adam responded, letting me follow his voice. "You need to run. Get away from here."

"We're leaving together." I argued, dropping to my knees.

"Leave me."

"I can't." I lost him once. I won't do it again.

"Eve."

"Don't argue with me."

Adam was sitting in a chair. Either he was too weak to move or tied to it. I ran my hands along his arm. There was rope wrapped around it. I couldn't see the loops and knots, making removing them challenging. I felt Noah join me on the ground.

"Let me help." He grumbled.

I shifted to give him more room and focused on the bindings on Adam's wrists. Noah moved a lot faster. By the time I freed a single wrist, Noah had freed Adam's legs. I knew this because I saw and heard his feet slide away from the chair legs into a more comfortable position.

"Who are you?" Adam asked.

"Our saviour." I responded.

"Seriously?" There was an edge to Noah's tone.

"Thank you." Adam stood and pulled me into his arms. "Let's get out of here."

I hugged Adam. It's been five years since I felt his touch. Five years is a long time. I didn't feel the same warmth with Adam as with Noah.

"The sooner, the better." I responded.

Noah hunched over, clutching at his chest. I pushed away from Adam to go to him, but he held me tight.

"What a touching scene."

I turned in Adam's arms to face the voice. Adam tucked me behind him. A useless act. He was released of her spell recently, but he'd still be weak to her magic. I was powerless against her magic. Noah might be the only one strong enough to resist her.

"Young love has been reunited." Rosetta spoke wistfully. "Yet heartbreak has taken such a strong wolf down."

"I'm not down." Noah growled.

Aiden's spell. It must have taken effect. But why now? I thought back. Noah's answers never seemed to make sense with what was being spoken. The hazy cloud. It has to be a spell that alters words. Noah must not have heard a thing I've said, only a twisted version Rosetta would have wanted him to hear.

"Excellent." Rosetta sounded happy. "Stay with me, and you'll never feel heartbroken again."

"No!" I shouted.

I went for Noah again, but Adam grabbed my arm, stopping me. I won't let Rosetta take another person in front of me again. Yanking my arm from Adam's grip, I grabbed Noah's arm. He was already walking toward Rosetta.

I tugged. He pulled free. I grabbed him again and tugged harder. Noah stumbled. I kept a tight grip on Noah, refusing to let him go. He turned to me, and I kissed him. I cupped his face and prayed I could break any spell Rosetta weaved onto him. He wrapped his arms around me and kissed me back. I relaxed into him. Now isn't the time to relax. I pushed at Noah's shoulder.

"Are you back?" I asked when I could speak.

"Back from where?" He asked.

"That witch almost had you under her spell."

"I can't hold this door much longer." Adam interrupted.

I pushed away from Noah to help Adam. We need another way out. Without my sight, I'd be useless. Noah is going to have to do it.

"What happened?" Noah asked.

Adam responded. "Rosetta manipulates the hearts of men."

"I know that much."

"Can we talk later?" I grumbled at the effort of trying to keep the door closed.

The banging on the other side of the door became more forceful. I'm not sure how much longer Adam and I can hold on.

"This way." Noah called.

Adam took my hand and pulled me toward to exit Noah found. We ran down a hall. It was dark. I could barely see what was around us. Adam stopped, letting me go. Noah whispered in my ear that we had to climb a ladder. Noah guided my hands to the rungs, then, when I was up a little higher, he pushed my jeans up and took hold of my ankle. I was able to see the rungs and climbed out with little difficulty. At the top, Adam took my hand and pulled me up. I lost Noah's touch.

"My car is parked at the edge of the driveway." Noah stated.

Noah and Adam began running away from our exit. I did start to follow but stopped and turned around. I can't just leave. Rosetta caused me too much pain, and I'm sure pain to many others as well. She has to be stopped once and for all. I returned to the dark hallway, retracing my steps to where Noah found me.

Rosetta was alone. I didn't see any other grey shape around her, and I couldn't smell anyone else. Not that my sense of smell could have helped me. Her strawberry champagne scent permeated the property.

"Eve." Rosetta cooed. "I knew you'd come back."

"We have some unfinished business."

"Indeed we do."

I felt Rosetta's magic as she prepared a spell. It pricked my skin — the attack spell landed by my feet. The last time we fought, I could see the trajectory of her magic. This time I'm at a huge disadvantage.

"You don't stand a chance." Rosetta threatened.

"We'll see about that." I retorted.

Rosetta's magic wrapped around her, creating a giant grey bubble in my vision. I couldn't see her form. A crackling sound was my only indicator that a spell had been cast. I couldn't see where it was coming from. A very subtle crackling from my right had me lunging to the left. I felt the heat of the spell as an explosion hit where I was standing.

To avoid the spells, I'll have to focus on my hearing. Now knowing how to proceed, I launched forward. Rosetta wouldn't let me get close — two steps forward, then four back. I refuse to give up.

"I don't know why you insist on continuing this futile attempt to get to me." Rosetta stated calmly.

"You caused me much grief, taking Adam away from me."

"You have him back."

Our talking distracted me, and a spell hit me in the leg. I fell to my knees. The attack felt like a thousand little needles were stabbing at my muscles.

"All you do is take." I growled. "Not caring about who you're hurting in the process."

I forced myself to my feet. Rosetta must be mad because the magic bubble grew and changed shape. Tendrils extended out, and the crackling became thunderous. I couldn't distinguish where the next spell would be coming from.

"You selfish little wolf." Rosetta bellowed. "Keeping all the love to yourself. You know nothing of true grief."

Rosetta's next spell was powerful. It hit me in the chest, lifted me off the ground, and slammed me into a wall. The air was knocked out of me with the impact. Her spell kept pushing on me harder. I could feel and hear my bones crunching. I couldn't move. The pain overwhelmed my senses.

The last thing I remember is a growl.

Chapter Nine

Noah

It's been two weeks since the incident. Eve was in Dr. Twin's care and still unconscious. In those two weeks, I've had the pack working hard to return Rosetta's victims to their homes after we destroyed all those jars. Her victims came from all over the world, and from over the years. Some don't have homes to return to. Aiden regained his heart. After a few days with Dr. Twin to ensure no lingering effects, he jumped in to help the other victims. I've been busy coordinating everything, and my mind wanders to Eve in the rare quiet moment.

"Alpha Noah."

I looked up from the paperwork I'd been buried in for the past two weeks. Adam stood in the doorway. He was joyfully welcomed back into the pack by those who knew him before he was taken. A lot has changed in the five years he was gone. He had a lot to learn. I don't think anyone has told him about his father yet.

"Noah, please." I leaned back. "What can I do for you, Adam?"

"I challenge you."

I raised a brow, studying him. He appeared serious about the request, but I'm uncertain about his reason. Pack law dictates that I have to accept any challenge unless there is an excellent reason why I should deny the challenge. I doubt he'd win anyway.

"Are you certain?" I questioned. "You've been back for such a short time."

"Are you defying pack law?" Adam countered.

I shook my head. "Just making sure you're challenging me for the right reasons."

Adam's eyes glowed yellow, and he straightened his shoulders. "I am."

"Very well." I stood. "Let's find Tate. He'll be our judge and witness."

Adam nodded and stepped back for me to pass. He walked next to me as we left the community center. Tate should be at the ranch managing horse riding lessons.

"Have you seen Eve?" I asked, finding the silence between us awkward.

"Every day." Adam said solemnly. "Dr. Twin has been keeping her unconscious until her bones healed. He removed that spell yesterday, so it's all up to her now."

"That's good to hear."

"When she wakes, I'll give her the life she deserves. I'll make up for the past five years."

I nodded. Adam doesn't deserve Eve, but that's not my choice. If Eve wants Adam, then I'll step back. My wolf huffed, not liking the idea of Eve with someone other than me, I don't like it either, but I can't force her to be with me. Well, I could, but it wouldn't be right. She's my mate, but if she doesn't choose to be with me, I must accept that I'll never have that sense of being whole. I feel complete when I'm with Eve.

"What about your father?" I changed the subject.

"What about him? You killed him when you became Alpha."

I stopped. "Who told you that?"

"No one." Adam shrugged. "Since no one spoke of him, I assumed you killed him during your challenge. Most Alpha challenges end in death."

"He left." Tate joined us outside the ranch. "Your father wasn't in the right mind to lead when you disappeared. Alpha Noah's challenge was fair."

"Oh." Adam looked sheepish.

"What are you doing here, Alpha?"

"Adam challenged me, and we need a judge."

Tate nodded and took the lead. There's an open field on the other side of pack land. It's used for sporting events, fairs, and challenges. Tate stood at the edge. Adam and I faced each other in the center of the field. Adam crouched, ready to attack. I spread my legs and hunched forward in preparation to tackle him. But that was only an illusion. My fighting style is strategic. My moves are calculated to counter any attack and to tire out my opponent so my attacks will knock them down.

Tate signalled the start of the challenge. Adam charged at me. When he was close, I moved out of the way. Adam's forward momentum took him further than he anticipated. It took him a bit to stop, seeing as he expected to slam into me. With a growl, he turned and tried again — with the same results.

"Coward."

"You're out of your league." I told him.

Adam shook his head. "I'm fighting for Eve, fighting for love."

I gritted my teeth. If his love for Eve were true, then he wouldn't have gotten caught up in Rosetta's spell. He abandoned her. Now, after five years, he wants her back like nothing happened. He will not win this challenge. I won't let him win.

Adam shifted strategies. He put his hands up like a boxer. I mimicked him. Adam swung first. I blocked his left jab, retaliating with a jab to the ribs. He bent into the pain, giving me an opening to throw another punch, this one to his face. Adam stumbled back but didn't fall. I went with an uppercut. Adam's head jerked back, and he stumbled away from me.

I watched and waited. Either Adam will reorient himself and try to land another blow. Or, if he's smart, he'll end this challenge. When he looked at me, the determination to win was still strong. I inwardly sighed and prepared to continue this challenge.

Adam's new round of attacks was faster than before. Almost like his previous attempts were only a test to see my reaction. He was pushing me back. I was blocking well enough that he couldn't lay a damaging blow, but I couldn't counter either. Adam brought his foot up in a high kick. I caught his leg on my shoulder and held on. Adam growled, trying to pull away, but on only one foot, he was off balance. I swept a leg under him. Still holding onto his leg, I went down with him. I shifted and pressed my forearm into his neck, pushing until Adam tapped out.

"Damn it!" Adam choked out, punching the ground.

"Tate?" I looked up at my Beta.

"Alpha Noah wins." He replied.

I helped Adam up. "Are you okay?"

"Fine." Adam grumbled. "Let's go again."

"Maybe you should rest up, or go visit your father."

"Later. I need to be Alpha before Eve wakes up."

"Why?" Tate questioned.

Adam stared at him like he just asked the world's dumbest question. "As Alpha, I can help her. She needs me."

Tate scowled. "Alpha Noah, you can deal with this child."

"Hey!"

Tate turned and started walking away.

"Don't turn your back on me!"

"Adam." I ran a hand through my hair. "Talk to Eve before making another challenge."

"She'll be thrilled. I'll be where I'm supposed to be. She'll be by my side. We'll lead the pack together." Adam urged. I wasn't sure if he was trying to convince me, or himself. "Just like we talked about."

"Five years ago." I reminded him. "Things have changed. She's changed. Like a child, you're only thinking of yourself."

"I'm thinking of Eve!"

"Being Alpha means thinking for the pack."

Adam's hands balled into fists. "I can do that as soon as Eve is at my side."

I wanted to grab his shoulders and shake some sense into him. He's trapped in a past that he wants to bring back. My cell phone rang. My brows knitted at the unknown number.

"Hello?"

"Noah. It's Will."

My heart tightened. "Is she awake?"

"A few minutes ago."

"Thank you, Will." My heart beat again, relieved over the good news. "I'm going to send Adam."

"Are you sure?"

"No." I chuckled bitterly. "But they have a past."

"Very well." Will stated. "Don't let her slip away."

I don't plan on it. I hung up and told Adam to go to her. He didn't hesitate. I want to be there, to hold her hand so I'm the first one she sees. As I told Will — Eve and Adam have a past. If I want Eve to be with me, she must first let go of her past. To do that, she and Adam have to talk.

"I saw Adam run off." Tate commented when I returned to the community center.

"Eve woke up."

"So you sent Adam."

I nodded.

"When Alpha Jack brought Eve into the pack, she was broken, abused by her previous Alpha." Tate explained, closing the door to the office so we were alone. "Adam fell for her hard and fast. He worked on opening her up and healing her broken soul. He was going to propose to her, but he disappeared. She tracked him down, but it was too late. He was gone. When Eve returned, broken, bruised, and blind, Alpha Jack blamed her for not being able to rescue his son and banished her from the pack."

Waves of emotions went through me. Anger, pain, pity, sadness. This is my first time hearing about Eve's past with the pack. Now I'm uncertain if sending Adam to her was the right thing to do.

"I didn't know a witch took Adam." Tate admitted. "She never told us. I know Julianne refused to abandon Eve. She was punished every time she was caught helping Eve. I think she knew the truth or at least more than the rest of us."

"Why wasn't Julianne banished?"

"She was dating Kevin, Adam's younger brother."

"I didn't realize Alpha Jack had two sons."

Tate grimaced. "He was obsessed with the eldest son and neglected the youngest."

"Why are you telling me all of this?"

"I saw you with Eve. She's your mate."

I stared at him dumbfounded. He sensed it too. "She's attractive."

He chuckled. "There were sparks."

"I'm not talking about this with you."

"Fine, but having a mate will make you stronger. Adam and Eve didn't spark the way you two do."

With that last statement, Tate left my office. If he saw it, then others must have too. All I need is for Eve to realize we're mates. I tried working, but the conversation with Tate ran in the back of my mind. I couldn't concentrate. Giving up, I went to visit Aiden.

"Noah." Aiden popped his head out of his apartment moments after I exited the elevator. He stepped aside letting me enter. "What are you doing here?"

"I came to check up on you."

"Uh-huh." He shook his head, disbelieving. "I'm doing good. It's like Rosetta's magic never affected me."

I grabbed a beer from the fridge. I could feel Aiden's gaze on my back. Taking a sip, I turned to him. "What?"

"Something is weighing on your mind."

With a heavy sigh, I grabbed him a beer too. He took it with a raised brow. I started from the beginning, with the reason I went to Eve up to today when I sent Adam to her. Aiden listened. He'd settled in on a bar stool. I couldn't stay still and paced the kitchen as I spoke.

"Tate says she's my mate." I finished.

"Is she your mate?" Aiden questioned. "I'm not a wolf. To me, it sounds like you love her."

"I don't know if I love her. I barely know her."

"You didn't answer my question."

"Yes, she's my mate."

"Is this why you're here? Because you wanted me to confirm that this infatuation you have for a woman you met a week ago is the one and only woman for you?"

I shook my head. "It's Adam."

"What about him?"

"He's her first love. She only helped me because it led her to him." I explained.

Aiden shook his head. "Sounded more like he was the first to love her. As for her apparent need to find him, I suspect it has more to do with guilt over love."

I voiced my concerns. "What if Eve still loves Adam and chooses him?"

"Then it's your fault for pushing Adam on her."

"I can't force her to be with me. I know she's my mate, but she may not feel the same thing for me."

I chugged the last of my beer. Indecision warring within me. Hold back and let Eve choose, or go to her and steer her my way. If I do either, I could lose her to another man or worry I had forced her to choose me when it's not what she wanted.

"The only way to know how Eve feels is to ask her." Aiden said as if reading my mind. "Be careful. You don't want to scare her away."

Chapter Ten

Eve

As my consciousness stirred, I opened my eyes and began to panic. My vision was black. I couldn't see. I must have made some noise because of a rush of fabric and footsteps heard somewhere nearby.

"Shh." I recognized Dr. Twin's voice. "You're okay, Darling."

Something was removed from my face, and I could see grey again. A calmness with its familiarity settled in. No longer panicked from losing even more of my vision, I began to feel every ache and pain in my body. My back, ribs, head. Every part of me ached.

"What happened?"

My voice came out raspy. I tried to sit up and sucked in a sharp breath. My ribs hurt the most. Dr. Twin's hands were gentle as he helped me into a sitting position. He propped pillows behind my back before turning away.

"Drink this."

He put what felt like a straw to my lips. I sucked. A cool liquid coated my throat. I couldn't describe its flavour but knew it wasn't water. When he was satisfied I'd drank enough, Dr. Twin pulled the straw away. The — I'm assuming bed — dipped as Dr. Twin sat beside me and took my hand.

"That potion should help to ease your pain." He explained.

"What happened?" I repeated, my voice no longer raspy after the potion.

"Noah brought you in two weeks ago. You were unconscious with broken ribs and other cracked bones."

"The witch!" I exclaimed in alarm as I remembered the spell that had slammed me into the concrete wall.

"Dead. Noah killed her."

That knowledge put me at ease. "Is Noah okay?"

"He's fine. I performed a check-up just to be sure."

Dr. Twin squeezed my hand reassuringly. "Aiden and Adam are also fine."

"Adam." I repeated the name softly.

"I have a few other patients to look after. You rest up. I'll come back to check on you later."

Dr. Twin kissed my forehead before I heard the door open and then close. Alone in the room, my thoughts and emotions took over. At least while I was talking, I could ignore it all.

Adam's back. Alpha Jack would be thrilled. Maybe he'll remove my banishment from the pack. That thought wasn't comforting. It was a little scary. Do I want to go back to the pack? They were so quick to turn their back on me. Except for Julianne, she never abandoned me. And I like my apartment. I don't think I'd enjoy living behind the horse ranch.

What about Noah? He was affectionate while I was looking for Aiden's heart. Was it just a ploy for an end game? My wolf chuffed at that line of thinking. Am I able to put myself in the care of another? I remembered Julianne's words about how I shouldn't stay in the past. Maybe Noah could be my mate. I feel differently when I am with him than I had with Adam. How do I even find my mate?

There was a soft knock at the door before it creaked open. "Eve?"

I looked at the door, unable to distinguish who stood there, but the voice sounded familiar. "Adam?"

"You're really awake." He let out a relieved sigh.

Adam's apple scent filled the room as I watched his grey form approach. He sat on the bed where Dr. Twin sat earlier and took my hand. He kissed it and then scooted closer.

"Your eyes." He brushed a thumb under one eye. "They are no longer hazel."

"The witch." I said in a way of explanation.

"It'll take some getting used to."

"Did Dr. Twin tell you I'm awake?"

"No." Adam said. "Noah was called. He told me to come."

My throat tightened. Maybe he doesn't want me. "Oh."

"I'm here."

"Alpha Jack must be thrilled to have you back."

Adam went silent for a moment. "My father is no longer Alpha. Noah is."

"Oh." I couldn't help the surprise in my tone. "I didn't know that."

"I've been told that my father was distraught over me disappearing, which is why Noah challenged him for Alpha."

"I'm sorry." I looked away, knowing most Alpha challenges end in death. "You're back, but your father isn't."

"Tate says my father is still alive, just no longer with the pack."

Knowing Noah didn't kill Alpha Jack to get the title of Alpha eased some tension in my shoulders. A tension I didn't realize had gathered there. Adam cupped my cheek and brushed his lips along mine, tentatively at first, before he pressed more firmly. I felt nothing. Noah's kiss was electrifying, and his touch was magical. I gripped Adam's wrist and pulled away.

"Enough about my father." Adam declared. "Let's talk about us."

"There is no us." I told him solemnly.

"Sure there is. I love you, Eve. We might have been apart for a few years, but we can get that time back. Get back to what we had."

"No, we can't, Adam." I pulled my hand from him, breaking all contact. "I thought that was what I wanted. That's why I helped Noah to find Aiden's heart. I knew it would lead me to you. Now that you're here, I can't go back."

"What do you mean?"

"A relationship with you would keep me in the past. It's been five years Adam. I've changed."

"Sure, your eyes are a different colour."

I let out a bitter laugh. "I'm blind, and Alpha Jack banished me from the pack because I lost you. I spent five years adapting to being alone and blind."

"I didn't know." Adam said softly.

"Of course not. You want to pick up where you left off. I can't do that."

"I'm sorry."

I blinked back tears. "When I tried to save you five years ago, Rosetta said our love wasn't strong enough. She was right."

"That can't be true."

"I couldn't break you of her spell, Adam. That broke me."

"Eve, I'm sorry."

"It wasn't until this moment did I realize the truth." I took a shaky breath. "I stopped loving you sometime in the five years you were gone. I needed to find you to redeem myself in front of Alpha Jack."

"Noah was right." Adam said bitterly.

That caught me off guard. "About what?"

"Never mind." Adam kissed my forehead, standing from the bed. "I'm really happy to see you. I hope you find the love that you deserve."

"Where are you going?"

"To see my father. He may need me more than you do."

The hurt in Adam's voice cut me. It also felt like a final goodbye, like I'll never see him again. I didn't want that, but I also didn't want to pick up where we left off. I need to move forward, and so does he. We were good for each other in the past, but there's now a five-year gap between us that we can't close.

Dr. Twin let me go home after a check-up. Aside from the ache in my upper body, my bones have healed. Will drove me home and helped me into my apartment.

My apartment felt cold and stuffy. There's the faintest scent of apples and pine – Adam and Noah's scent. My heart tightened, and my throat closed. I need to clear my apartment of their scent. Going to the living room, I opened a window.

From outside, the scent of pizza wafted up. It made my stomach growl. Patting my pockets, I realized my cell phone was missing. Where did I lose it? I'll need Julianne to help me get a new one. For now, Mrs. Zaw will let me use her phone.

I opened the door, intending to cross the hall, and stepped back. Noah's light grey figure stood in the hall, and based on the scent, he held a pizza box.

"Eve." Noah whispered my name, almost in awe.

"Noah." I couldn't believe he was here.

"Can I come in? I have pizza."

I opened the door wider. "I'll accept the pizza."

He chuckled, stepping into my apartment. Locking the door, I followed Noah to the living room. I watched him bend to place the box on the table and then move to the kitchen. The sound of ceramic told me he was grabbing plates. Noah sat on the couch. The scent of pizza amplified when he opened the box.

"Come sit."

"Is that an order, Alpha?"

He went silent. I wished I could see him. See the expression I'm sure he made. Or maybe I don't.

"How long have you known?" He asked, his voice strained.

"Since earlier today. Adam told me." I took a seat on the couch with him. "Why didn't you?"

"I was going to. At first, it didn't matter because it had no relevance to finding Aiden's heart. Then I started to get the impression you were scared of the Alpha, and I didn't want you scared of me." Noah's hand hovered over mine before he drew it back. "Tate told me what Alpha Jack did to you, how he and the pack treated you. I was going to tell you I'm Alpha because I want you to know I'm different."

I picked up a slice of pizza, trying to figure out how to respond. If he'd told me he was Alpha from the beginning, I may not feel hurt right now. I definitely wouldn't have let him get so close. I consumed a whole slice, the silence between us thick as I contemplated Noah's actions.

"Maybe I should go." Noah finally stated.

"Stay." I reached out and took his hand.

"Are you sure?"

I nodded. "I wish you'd told me you are Alpha instead of hearing it from Adam first."

"I'm sorry." Noah squeezed my hand. "Where is Adam anyway? I thought he'd be here with you."

"He went to see his father."

"That's good."

I looked at Noah for the first time tonight. His green eyes were steady on me, concern clear in his gaze. Worry about what, I'm not sure. I studied his face. I like his eyes. They are gentle and loving. His light brown hair is a little long, and he has the start of a beard. He looks tired and worn out. I wanted to reach out and run my fingers through his hair, wanted to cup his cheek and kiss him, but I resisted the urge. I need to know how he feels about me.

"I doubt he's coming back." I blurted.

"What makes you say that?"

"I broke up with him. Officially."

Noah frowned. "Is that what you wanted?"

I shifted closer to him. "Yes."

A slow smile graced his features. Butterflies fluttered in my gut. Am I making myself clear enough? Noah raised his free hand to cup my cheek. The gentle gesture was not reassuring to my nerves. I've never flirted before, I've never had to. I am not sure I'm doing this right.

"Tell me, Eve, were you happy with Adam?"

I frowned. That's not what I was expecting him to ask. I wanted him to lean in and kiss me. To tell me he won't leave me. Just like he did last time he was over. I want to know if he meant it.

Noah let go of my hand. He cupped the back of my neck, maintaining skin-to-skin contact as he hoisted me onto his lap. I let out a little yelp of surprise. My wolf pranced around in my mind, thrilled by the close contact. I kept my hands on my lap, uncertain what to do with them.

"I need you to do something for me." Noah said.

"What?" I asked meekly.

"Find a heart." He grinned. "I seemed to have lost mine."

I stared at him, not entirely understanding his words. Noah waited. When my mind finally understood, I smiled.

"A heart is not easy to find. Where did you last see it?"

"In the hands of a beautiful woman with the most stunning stormy eyes. I think she may have stolen it."

I beamed at the compliment. "What if I can't find it?"

"I believe you can." He brushed his lips along mine.

"Do you want your heart back?"

"She can keep it if she'll give me hers."

"Deal."

With that final word, Noah kissed me. I wrapped my arms around Noah's neck, not wanting to let go. My wolf settled in my mind, perfectly content. I can see a bright future for the first time in five years. I have no fear over what's to come with Noah at my side.

About the Author

Ivy Marie grew up an army brat. Moving every two or three years, and finally settling in Ottawa, Ontario, Canada. When she's not writing she's at work, or spending time with her friends.

Both friends and family are supportive of her creative expression. She's found comfort in Supernatural Romance, with werewolves and vampires as the main creatures she writes about, and also in Contemporary Romance.

Ivy Marie writes for her own enjoyment. She also hopes that the joy she feels while writing is expressed and passed on to you.

Connect

I really appreciate you reading my book! Here are my social media coordinates;

Facebook: www.facebook.com/IvysStolenHearts
Instagram: ivymariebooks
Blue Sky: @ivymarie-author.bsky.social
X: @IvyMarie_Books
Website: www.ivymarieauthor.com

Don't forget about my wonderful cover artist - Shawna Russ;

Instagram: shawncolourart

Also By

Keep an eye out other books by Ivy Marie.

Contemporary Romance
Thief in Paris
Bad Decisions (Book 1 of Decisions Duet)
Late Decisions (Book 2 of Decisions Duet)
Surprised by Love ~ Coming 2025
Fan the Flames ~ Coming 2026

Paranormal Romance
Stolen Heart
His Hunter
Bound to the Reaper (Book 1 of Reaper)
Reaper Undercover (Book 2 of Reaper) ~ Coming 2026
Reaper Forever (Book 3 of Reaper) ~ Coming 2027
Witch Troubles ~ Coming 2025

Like Hell series (Paranormal Romance) ~ Coming 2028

Like Hell Mario (Prequel)

Like Hell this is Real (Book 1)

Like Hell this is Normal (Book 2)

Like Hell this is Happening (Book 3)

Like Hell Alternative (Alternate Reality)